Jason stood quite close to her, his hair rumpled and colour slashing his cheekbones.

He braced his hands against the wall on either side of her head, so that she was effectively imprisoned, although standing between the strength of his arms did not feel like being trapped. Instead, as her heart started to pound and her cheeks flushed, Emily felt a glorious sense of anticipation rise up inside her like a bubble. She felt almost as if she could float right off the ground, anchored only by the heavy thud of her heart. Jason's gaze remained on her, his eyes the color of dark honey, and Emily could not look away.

From somewhere she found words. She gave him a pointed look, meaning to end the conversation and dismiss him. "Just what is it you'd like to do?"

"This."

As he lowered his head to hers, a part of Emily's befuddled brain wondered what on earth he intended to do—while another, shocked part, acknowledged, *He's going to kiss me.*

The Powerful and the Pure
When Beauty tames the brooding Beast...

From Mr. Darcy to Heathcliff, the best romantic
heroes have always been tall,
dark and *dangerously* irresistible.

This year, indulge yourself as Harlequin Presents®
brings you four formidable men—the ultimate heroes.
Untamable...or so they think!

**Make sure to pick up these four
timeless love stories!**

Available wherever Harlequin books are sold
or online at Harlequin.com

Kate Hewitt

THE MATCHMAKER BRIDE

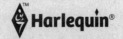

TORONTO NEW YORK LONDON
AMSTERDAM PARIS SYDNEY HAMBURG
STOCKHOLM ATHENS TOKYO MILAN MADRID
PRAGUE WARSAW BUDAPEST AUCKLAND

Recycling programs
for this product may
not exist in your area.

ISBN-13: 978-0-373-23772-2

THE MATCHMAKER BRIDE
Previously published in the U.K. under the title MR AND MISCHIEF

First North American Publication 2011

Copyright © 2011 by Kate Hewitt

THE MATCHMAKER BRIDE

To Meg.

Thank you for years of wonderful advice and encouragment, and helping me to make my books the best they can be.

CHAPTER ONE

'IT LOOKS like I missed the party.'

Emily Wood turned from her rather dour perusal of the leaving-party detritus, surprised that anyone was left. Stephanie had gone an hour ago, full of high spirits and plans for her wedding in a month's time, and the rest of the employees had trickled away afterwards, leaving nothing but a few tables of crumb-scattered plates and glasses of now-flat champagne in the office's party room.

'Jason!' The name burst from her lips as she stared in surprise at the man lounging against the doorway. 'You're back!'

'My plane landed an hour ago,' Jason replied, glancing ruefully around at the mess. 'I thought I might make the end of the party, but obviously I was mistaken.'

'Just in time for the clean-up,' Emily replied lightly. She crossed the room and, standing on her tiptoes, reached up to kiss his cheek. 'How lovely to see you.' His skin was warm and she inhaled the citrusy tang of his aftershave; the scent was more pungent than one she would have associated with stoic, straight-as-an-arrow Jason, the boy who had kept her out of trouble, the man who had left Highfield for a high-profile career in civil engineering. He was her boss and oldest family friend, although whether he was *her* friend was another matter altogether. Looking at his rather cool expression now, Emily remembered how Jason always seemed to disapprove of her just a bit.

She stepped back with a brisk smile. Jason hadn't moved, but Emily was gratified to see the tiniest quirk of his mouth. Amazing, but it almost looked like a smile. 'I didn't know you were due back in London.' As founder and CEO of Kingsley Engineering, Jason travelled for most of the year. Emily couldn't even remember the last time she'd seen him beyond a flash of sober suit in the hall-way, or amidst the chaos of a family gathering back in Surrey. He'd certainly never sought her out like this.

Although, she acknowledged as she began to gather up the icing-smeared plates, he wasn't really seeking her out. He'd just missed the party.

'I thought it was about time I came home,' Jason said. He glanced around at the empty tables. 'It looks like it was a successful party. But then, of course, I wouldn't expect anything less.'

Successful, Emily thought, rather than *fun*. So typical of Jason. She arched her eyebrows. 'Oh, and why is that?'

'You're quite the busy little socialite, Em.'

Emily bristled, because the words did not sound complimentary coming out of Jason's mouth. Just because she enjoyed a party hardly made her some kind of scatty socialite. And the childhood nickname surprised her, even though it shouldn't. Jason had been the only one to call her that. Little Em, he'd tease, yanking her plaits and giving her a smile that wasn't quite condescending. More just…knowing. Yet he could hardly say he knew her now; despite working for his company, with his intense travel schedule she'd barely seen him in the five years she'd been at KE. And she couldn't remember the last time he'd called her Em.

'I wasn't aware you kept tabs on my social activities,' she said, only half-joking.

'I'm honour bound to, considering our history. And, in any case, you've made the social pages enough it would be hard not to notice.'

Emily gave him a playful smile. 'And you read the social pages?'

'I eagerly await them every morning.'

Emily burst out laughing, for the thought of Jason poring over photos of ageing debutantes and profligate playboys was utterly ludicrous, though she'd hardly expect him to joke about it—or joke about anything, really. More than once she'd wondered if he'd had his sense of humour surgically removed.

'Actually,' he continued, his tone serious and even

severe once more, 'my PA scans them for me. I need to know what my employees are up to.'

Ah, there he was. The real Jason, the Jason she knew and remembered, always ready to deliver a scolding or shoot her one of those stern looks. Emily gave him a sunny smile. 'Well, as you can see, this was quite the wild party. Cake and streamers, and I believe someone *might* have brought out the karaoke machine. Scandalous.'

'Don't forget the champagne.'

Emily reached for several empty plastic flutes. 'How did you guess?'

'Actually, I provided it.'

'You did?' She couldn't keep the surprise from her voice, and Jason's mouth quirked again in a small smile. He propped one shoulder against the doorway.

'Really, Emily, I'm not quite that stern a taskmaster. And I did actually try to make it to this party. Stephanie has been with the company for over five years.'

'Ah, so that's the reason. You probably give out some kind of honorary plaque.'

'You only get one of those for ten years' service,' Jason told her, and Emily's mouth dropped open. He had to be kidding—then she saw a telltale glint in his eyes and realised he was. Two jokes in one day. What had happened to him in Africa?

Surprised and a little discomfited by their banter, Emily paused in her clearing up to look at him properly; he wore a suit—of course—of expensive grey silk, a muted navy tie knotted at his throat. His hair, chocolate brown, the same colour as his eyes, was cut short. He looked crisp and clean and neat, remote and untouchable with that small, rather superior smile Emily had never completely liked but accepted as part of who Jason was, the exalted older brother-in-law, separated from her by twelve years, distant and just a little disapproving.

He'd never taken part in their silly childhood games. She, her sister Isobel, and Jason's younger brother Jack had always got into the most amazing scrapes, and Jason had been the one to bail them out and lecture them afterwards. She'd accepted and resented it at turns, yet never questioned his innate authority. It was too much a part of him, and the relationship he'd had with them all. Yet it had been months since she'd seen him, years since they'd really talked.

Five years ago, when she'd arrived in London looking for a job, he'd directed her to Stephanie, then Head of Human Resources, and then barely seen her settle in as a secretary before he'd been off again, directing a building project in Asia. The times he'd seen her since then had been at the office, where he kept a cool, professional distance, or back in Surrey at various family gatherings, where he was no more than what he'd always been—Jason, as good as an older brother, bossy and perhaps a little bit boring but still…Jason. An essential part of the landscape of her life, steady and staid and *there*.

'So are you back for long this time?' she asked, turning back to the table of paper plates.

'A few months I hope. I have some business locally to take care of.' He spoke casually enough, yet Emily sensed an undercurrent of intensity that sparked her curiosity, and she glanced back at him. Jason's impassive face gave nothing away.

'Local business?' she repeated as she dumped another load of paper plates into the bin. 'I didn't know KE had a local project going on.' As a civil engineer, Jason's speciality was water management in Third World countries. It was a rather impressive line Emily trotted out when conducting interviews, although she'd yet to really understand just what it entailed. He'd never done a local project before, as far as she knew.

'It's not to do with the company,' Jason replied, his voice mild.

'Personal business?' she asked. 'You mean family?' She thought of Jason's taciturn father, his tearaway brother, now married to her own sister. Was someone in trouble or ill? Her brow furrowed, and Jason's mouth quirked once more in that knowing little smile as he shook his head.

'You're full of questions, aren't you? No, as a matter of fact, it's nothing to do with family. But *personal*.' He stressed it lightly yet pointedly, making her feel a bit like the bratty little girl she'd undoubtedly been to his very cool teenager. Or twenty-something. He'd always been a little god-like in his maturity and sophistication. When she'd been getting braces, he'd already started his own company and made his first million.

'Sorry. I'll stop.' She smiled just as teasingly back, determined to keep it light and breezy, although now her curiosity was well and truly whetted. What kind of personal business could Jason Kingsley have? There had always been a fair amount of office speculation about the boss's personal life, for while he was in London he always had a different woman on his arm at various social functions, usually someone glamorous and shallow, and in Emily's opinion totally unsuitable for Jason. Yet she'd never seen him with a serious girlfriend and, despite the office's occasional forays into speculation about that aspect of their employer, Emily hadn't given too much thought to Jason's personal life. Of course, she'd hardly seen him at all. And although their families were intertwined through the marriage of her older sister to Jason's younger brother, he hardly ever went back to Highfield, the village in Surrey where they'd both grown up. And he'd already said it wasn't family-related, so what was it?

After another few seconds of silent speculation, Emily shrugged it aside. Clearly Jason's personal business had nothing to do with her. It was probably something incredibly boring, like taking care of an old debt or an ingrown toenail. She thought of Jason sitting on a doctor's examining table, and a sudden, bizarre image of him in nothing more than one of those awful little paper robes flashed across her brain. The mental picture was both ridiculous and yet strangely enthralling, for her overactive imagination seemed to have a rather good idea of what Jason's bare chest would look like.

An unexpected bubble of laughter erupted from her and she clapped her hand over her mouth. Jason glanced at her, shaking his head. 'You've always been able to see the lighter side of life, haven't you?' he said dryly, and she dropped her hand from her mouth to dazzle him with her brightest smile.

'It's a great talent of mine, although it takes some work in certain company.' His eyes narrowed and her smile widened. She knew Jason disapproved of her breezy attitude. She still remembered how sceptical he had looked when she'd come to London and asked him for a job. In retrospect, she *had* been a bit scatty, blithely assuming that Jason would have something for her to do, and pay her for it as well, but still it had been all too clear just how much Jason had doubted her capabilities.

You're here to work, Emily, not for a lark…

Well, she hoped she'd proved herself in that area at least over the last five years. She was poised to become the youngest Head of Human Resources the company had ever had—admittedly there had only been two before her—and Jason himself had suggested her promotion, according to Stephanie.

Despite that, as she looked back at him watching her with that knowing little smile, his eyes crinkled at the corners and she couldn't help but still feel like the silly young girl she'd once been. And, despite the promotion, he apparently still thought she was.

'So Stephanie is to be married in a month,' Jason mused. 'This Timothy fellow—he's all right?'

'He's lovely,' Emily said firmly. 'I had a hand in getting them together, actually.'

Jason arched an eyebrow, coolly sceptical as always. 'Really?'

'Yes, really,' she replied, slightly nettled. 'Tim is a friend of a friend of Isobel's, and she told me that Annie told her—'

'This is sounding far too complicated.'

'For you, perhaps,' Emily shot back. 'I found it quite simple. So Annie said—

'Give me the condensed version,' Jason cut her off, and Emily rolled her eyes.

'Oh, very well. I invited them both out to a party—'

'Now that part I have no trouble following.'

'Actually, it was a charity fund-raiser,' Emily informed him. 'For terminally ill children. In any case, they met there and—'

'And it was love at first sight, was it?' he filled in mockingly, and Emily pursed her lips.

'No, of course not. But they never would have even met if I hadn't arranged it, and in point of fact

Tim was a bit shy after his wife died, and Steph has an absolute horror of blind dates, so—'

'It took a bit of handholding?'

'Or helping them to hold each other's hands. You can't make someone love you, of course—'

'I should think not.'

Emily glanced at him curiously, for there was a sudden, darker note to Jason's tone she didn't expect or understand. She shrugged it aside. 'In any case, they're getting married in a month, so it all worked out nicely.'

'Very nicely indeed.' Jason had closed the space between them so she inhaled the citrusy whiff of his aftershave once more, felt the sudden heat of his body, and a strange new awareness prickled along her bare arms and up her spine. He really was awfully close.

'You have icing in your hair,' he said, and reached out to brush a sticky strand away from her cheek. His fingers were cool, the touch as light as a whisper, yet Emily stiffened in surprise anyway. She was conscious of how dishevelled she must look, with her hair falling down and a coffee stain on her skirt. Definitely not at her best.

She laughed lightly and pushed the unruly tendrils behind her ears. 'Yes, I'm rather a mess, aren't I? I just need to finish this clearing up.'

'You could leave it for the cleaning lady.'

'Alice? She's taken the day off.'

'You know her name?'

'I am about to become the Head of HR,' Emily reminded him. 'Her mother's ill and she's gone to Manchester for the weekend to see her settled in a care home. It was a terrible wrench for her to make the decision, of course, but I think it will work out—'

'I'm sure,' Jason murmured, effectively cutting her off yet again, and Emily gave him a knowing look.

'So sorry to bother you with details, but I thought you kept tabs on your employees' lives? Or just the ones who make the social pages?'

'I'm more concerned about how a social scandal reflects on Kingsley Engineering,' Jason replied, 'rather than the hows or whys of a cleaning lady taking the day off for her elderly mum.' He gestured for her to keep speaking. 'But do go on. It's fascinating how you take such an interest in other people's lives.'

Emily felt herself flush. Was that a criticism? And while she'd been high-spirited on occasion, she'd never involved herself in an actual scandal. Although she supposed high-spirited and scandal were synonymous in Jason's view. 'I suppose,' she told him rather pointedly, 'it's what makes me good at HR.'

'Absolutely, among other things.' He smiled, a proper one, not just a little quirk of his lips, revealing a dimple in one cheek. She'd forgotten about that dimple, forgotten when Jason smiled properly his eyes turned the colour of honey. They were normally brown, just as his hair was brown. Brown and boring. Except when he smiled. Abruptly, Emily turned back to the table. She could tell Jason was watching her, felt his assessing gaze sweep over her. Strange, how you could *feel* someone watching you.

'Are you planning Stephanie's wedding, as well?' he asked now. 'Some big fancy do?'

Emily turned around, brushing another unruly strand of hair from her eyes. 'The wedding? Heavens, no. That's far above my capabilities. And she's having it back home where she grew up.'

'But you'll be there, won't you? Maid of honour, I suppose?'

'As a matter of fact, yes.'

Jason's smile deepened, and so did his dimple. Something flashed in his eyes, something dark and unsettling. 'And you'll dance, won't you? At the wedding?' His voice had dipped to a husky murmur, a tone Emily didn't think she'd ever heard him use before, a tone that brushed across her senses with a shiver. She frowned, then froze as she realised just what Jason was alluding to with that little murmured remark.... Jack and Isobel's wedding, when they'd danced, and she had been seventeen years old and very, very silly. In the seven years since that episode had occurred, Jason had never mentioned it. Neither had she. She'd assumed he'd forgotten it—just as she had. Almost…until now. Now it was suddenly taking up far too much space in her brain.

'Of course,' she said after a moment, her voice light. She decided to ignore any implication he might have been making. They hardly needed to talk about that unfortunate episode now. 'I love to dance.' She glanced at him again and, despite her now almost twenty-five years, she felt every inch the gauche girl she'd been at that wedding. She'd made *such* a fool of herself, but at least she could laugh about it now. She *would* laugh about it.

'I know,' Jason said, his voice still no more than a murmur. 'I remember how we danced.' The corner of his mouth quirked up again, only for a second, as his gaze held hers. His eyes really were the most amazing colour…like whisky, or chocolate, but with golden glints.… 'Don't you?' he pressed, a lilt of challenge in his voice.

So he was going to mention it—and make her mention it, as well. From that knowing glint in his eyes, he intended to tease her about it, although why he'd waited seven years to do so, Emily had no idea. She smiled wryly, determined to ride it out. 'Ah, yes. How could I forget?' Jason didn't say anything, and Emily shook her head, rolling her eyes as if it was no more than an amusing little anecdote. It *was* a silly enough episode, seven years in the past, and surely it had no power to embarrass her now, even if she'd been mortified at the time.

It was just, Emily told herself, that they'd never

talked about it, not when he'd hired her, not when he'd kissed her cheek at their niece's baptism, nor when he'd sat at the far end of the table at Christmas dinner. On all of those occasions he'd remained rather remote, and only now was Emily realising how glad she'd been to retain that little distance. Yet here he was now, standing so close, bringing up all these memories, and behaving in a very un-Jasonlike way. It unnerved her.

She let out a light little laugh and gave him a self-mocking smile. 'I made quite an idiot of myself over you.'

Jason arched an eyebrow. 'Is that how you remember it?'

Of course he wouldn't make it easy for her. He never did. Not when she was six, not when she was seventeen, and not even now she was almost twenty-five. She should be used to his lightly mocking smiles, the eloquent arch of a single eyebrow, but somehow with the distance in their professional relationship she'd forgotten. She'd forgotten how much he could affect her.

'You don't remember?' she asked, pretending to shudder. 'That's a relief, I suppose.'

Jason didn't speak for a moment, and Emily busied herself with organising the dirty cutlery into a tidy pile. 'I remember,' he finally said, quietly, without any humour at all, and she felt a strange, icy thrill all the way down her spine.

And suddenly, without either of them saying

anything more, Emily felt as if that memory was right there with them, living and breathing and taking all the air. She certainly remembered it, could feel even now how young and happy she'd been—and so very silly.

Jason had asked her to dance, the obvious and polite thing to do since he was the brother of the groom and she the sister of the bride. He'd been a worldly twenty-nine to her naive seventeen years, and she'd been breathless and giddy from three glasses of champagne when he'd taken her in his arms and led her in a gentle and unthreatening waltz. It had been a dance of duty, and Emily had known it for what it was—she hadn't even *wanted* to dance with boring Jason Kingsley in the first place. All he'd ever really done was tease her or scold her.

Yet somehow, when he'd taken her in his arms, keeping her a safe six inches from his body, she'd felt something else. Something new and tingly and really quite nice, in a disquieting sort of way. She'd been an innocent at seventeen, and had never felt that sweet rush before. And so, despite Jason's serious expression and boring waltz, she'd tipped her head up and smiled at him with as much flirtatious charm as she thought she might ever possess and said, 'You're quite handsome, you know.'

Jason had looked down at her, his face so aggravatingly solemn. His expression hadn't changed one bit. 'Thank you.'

Somehow Emily didn't think that was what he

was supposed to have said. She wasn't sure of the script, yet she knew she didn't like these lines. And yet he *had* been handsome, with his dark hair and eyes, the white of his smile and the strength of his arms as he held her that proper distance away from his body. She could still feel the heat and strength of him and, fuelled by the champagne fizzing through her veins, Emily had added, 'Perhaps you'd like to kiss me.' She'd tilted her pretty little chin up further, and had even had the audacious stupidity to pucker her lips and wait. She'd let her eyelids flutter closed, so suddenly desperate to have him kiss her. It would have been her first kiss, and at that moment she'd wanted it so very much. She'd wanted Jason, which was ridiculous because she'd never once thought of Jason that way—never even considered such a possibility—until he'd asked her to dance.

The moment had gone on too long, several seconds that had made agonising awareness, as well as a punishing sobriety, steal over Emily. She'd opened her eyes and seen Jason gazing down at her in what was almost a glare. His eyes had narrowed, his mouth had tightened, and he hadn't looked friendly—or boring—at all. All of her flirtatiousness had drained out of her, leaving her as flat and stale as the dregs of her own champagne. She'd almost felt afraid.

Then his expression had changed, the glare wiped clean away, and he'd smiled faintly and said, 'I would, rather. But I won't.' And with that, before the dance had ended or even really started, he'd set her gently and firmly from him and walked off the dance floor.

Emily had stood there for several seconds, unmoving and incredulous. The public humiliation of being left on the dance floor was bad enough, but far worse was the private humiliation of being so summarily rejected by Jason Kingsley. She'd been quite sure, at that moment, that he really wouldn't want to kiss her. And because she'd been seventeen, tipsy, and it would have been her first kiss, she hadn't been able to lift her chin and throw her shoulders back and saunter off the dance floor like she'd meant to. Instead she'd stumbled across the parquet, dissolving into drunken tears before she'd even left the ballroom.

Definitely an idiot.

She turned to smile brightly at him now, forcing the memory—and its accompanying mortification—back to the far recesses of her brain. 'Well, I shan't ask you to dance again, I promise you,' she assured him. 'Never fear.'

A smile flickered across Jason's face like a wave of water. His gaze rested on her thoughtfully, as if he were taking her measure. 'But, Em, I was counting on you to ask me to dance.'

Slightly thrown, Emily laughed and replied, 'Well then, I certainly won't ask you to kiss me.'

'Then I shall be especially disappointed,' Jason returned, his voice soft, and Emily felt shock slice through her, rendering her quite speechless, until she realised that of course Jason was just teasing her, the same as always. Except he'd never teased her quite like that before.

Jason watched as shock widened Emily's jade-green eyes, her tongue darting out to moisten her lower lip. He felt a sudden jolt of desire at the sight of that innocent little action, and it both surprised and annoyed him. He had no business feeling that way about Emily…again.

He hadn't even meant to seek her out tonight. He had only a few months to be in London, and spending time with Emily Wood was low down on his list of priorities. In fact, *not* spending time with her was a priority. He had other more suitable women to pursue. Women who were sensible, level-headed and businesslike, perfect for his purpose. Emily, with her cat's eyes and teasing smile and endless legs, was definitely not any of those things. Even more importantly, she was off-limits. She'd been off-limits seven years ago, and she was still off-limits now—for more reasons than he cared to name or number.

'How does it feel to be the Head of Human Resources?' he asked, determined to move the conversation back to business. 'Youngest in the post.'

'Strange,' Emily admitted. 'I hope I'm up to the task.'

'I'm sure you will be.' He'd watched her grow into her position in HR from afar, and he'd been both surprised and encouraged by the way she'd taken to the role. Her promotion had been a smart business move, even though some—including Emily herself—might think it hinted at nepotism. Jason never let feelings get in the way of business. Or of anything.

'As for your first duty,' he told her, 'there's a woman I'd like you to interview on Monday, for a receptionist position.'

Emily glanced at him rather sharply. 'Oh?' she asked, her tone a bit diffident.

'Helen Smith. She's just come to London and could use a bit of help.'

'A friend of yours?' Emily asked, her voice sharpening just a little, and Jason suppressed a smile. Sometimes Emily was so easy to read. Could she actually be jealous? Did she still harbour a bit of the adolescent affection she'd shown him seven years ago?

The possibility was intriguing...and dangerous.

He still remembered the moment she'd tilted her pretty face up to his and said, *'Perhaps you'd like to kiss me.'*

And he *had* wanted to, more than he'd been willing to admit, even to himself.

That sudden, fierce jolt of lust had nearly knocked Jason to his knees. She'd been seventeen, practically a child, completely innocent and utterly naive. The strength of his own response had shocked and shamed him; he'd left the wedding immediately afterwards, near trembling with the aftershocks of surprising and suppressed desire, determined to put Emily completely from his mind.

And he'd accomplished just that, almost forgetting her completely, until three years later when she'd traipsed merrily to London without a plan—or a job—and he'd reluctantly offered her an entry level post.

He remembered how she'd sprawled in the chair across from his desk, her honey-blonde hair tumbling over her shoulders, her green cat's eyes alight with mischief. She'd worn an indecently short miniskirt and a top in a vivid green that matched her eyes; he suspected she considered such an outfit business attire. He couldn't keep his eyes off her long tanned legs, or the way one foot swung back and forth, a spiked heel dangling from her scarlet-polished toe.

Jason had stood behind his desk, his hands shoved in his pockets, doing his best to appear stern and disapproving. She'd been only twenty at the time and had looked artless and beautiful and so very young. And while he'd managed to forget how Emily had affected him three years ago, it had come back to him then with an overwhelming rush of memory and feeling.

'You can have me do anything,' she'd told him. 'I'm not fussed.' He'd stood there, looking grim, trying not to let it show on his face just what he could imagine having her do. It had been three years since they'd danced at the wedding, three years when he'd barely seen or thought of her at all, and yet he'd still felt that fierce dart of lust. When she'd leaned forward her hair had swung around her face and he'd smelled the scent of her shampoo. Strawberry.

She'd looked up at him from underneath her lashes, her eyes dancing with amusement. 'Honestly, Jason, you look positively dire! I'm not that bad, I assure you.'

From somewhere he'd summoned a smile. 'And whatever I have you do—I assume you want payment for it?'

She'd looked momentarily thrown, her expression unguarded and vulnerable, and with a stab of self-loathing he'd realised again just how young and inexperienced—in every way—she was. Then she'd laughed, a rich, throaty gurgle that had made Jason shove his hands even deeper into his pockets, a scowl marking his face. Emily had the laugh of an experienced woman, a sexy, sultry laugh, and it *did* things to him. When had she started laughing like that? When had she started to really grow up?

'Well, yes, that was the idea,' she said, smiling with that artless honesty that exasperated and endeared her to him at the same time.

And so he'd given her the post, as she'd undoubtedly known he would, and then he'd kept his distance. He'd had no intention of involving himself with an innocent like Emily, especially considering how their families were related. And he'd succeeded…until now. Now, when he'd seen her in the party room, wearing a candy-pink business suit that was so short it nearly showed her bottom when she bent to pick up a bit of rubbish from the floor. He'd stared at her, noticing the long, tanned length of her legs, the way that ridiculously short skirt moulded over her curves.

He should have walked away before she'd seen him. God knew he'd done it before. Yet something had compelled him to come into the room, and he'd spoken. Stayed. Seeing Emily after so long had been like finally finding a drink in the desert. Her warmth and humour had reached out to him, enveloped him and made him want more. And so he'd remained, joked and flirted, and then most damaging and dangerous of all, he'd mentioned that almost-kiss they'd shared seven years ago. Jason could not fathom why he'd done that, when he'd been perfectly happy never to think about it again, much less talk about it.

And surely Emily felt the same way…unless she did still have some vestige of that schoolgirl crush? The thought should alarm him, but it accomplished something else entirely. He wanted to watch her eyes darken to moss and see her tongue swipe at that lush mouth once more.

Annoyance prickled through him yet again. He needed to get a grip. This was Emily. *Emily.* Inappropriate, unsuitable and off-limits. Full stop.

'Helen Smith,' Emily repeated, and Jason could

tell she'd recovered her equanimity. 'I'll keep an eye out for her CV—'

'My PA emailed it to you this afternoon.'

'I see.' She gave him a quick, curious glance from under her lashes and then turned away. 'I'll make a note of it.'

'Good.' He was determined to keep the rest of their conversation purely professional, even as his gaze rested on the falling-down chignon of her glorious golden hair, one curling tendril resting on the curve of her breast. Determinedly, Jason yanked his gaze away, his mouth settling into a grim line, yet something still compelled him to add, 'I've never met her, actually. She's a friend of a friend, and I'd like to help her out. She should be suitable for an entry level position.' Why on earth was he explaining himself? There was absolutely no need.

'Fine,' Emily said briskly. 'I'll do what I can.'

'Good.' Jason matched her brisk tone and then gave one more glance around the cleaned-up room. He still had several phone calls and emails to answer, as well as a charity fund-raiser to attend. All part of the personal business Emily was so curious about… and which he had no intention of telling her.

She would, he thought with a grim twist of his mouth, find out soon enough.

Jason was looking grim again, which was a good thing, Emily decided. For a few moments there he'd seemed like someone else entirely, and the thought unsettled her. Her reaction had unsettled her even more, because when Jason had dropped his voice to that husky murmur and actually said he'd be *disappointed*...

Quickly, Emily pulled that train of thought to a screeching halt. Not something she needed to think about. At all. She glanced around the empty room with satisfaction, making sure her gaze was averted from Jason, and then went to turn off the lights.

She hadn't realised how dark it had become, twilight stealing softly over the city, so that the room was pitched into sudden darkness when she flicked the switch.

'Oops...' She laughed a little as she stood there in the dark, conscious how a lack of light made things seem almost...intimate. She could hear the gentle sound of Jason's breathing, and when she groped for the switch again she came into contact with Jason's chest instead, a hard wall of muscle that tensed against the flat of her palm. She hadn't realised he'd come so close. She jerked her hand away as a matter of instinct, even though the feel of that hard wall of muscle seemed to have imprinted itself on her palm. The last thing she wanted was Jason to think she was throwing herself at him... again.

'Sorry,' she muttered, yet she still didn't move. Her brain and body both seemed to have frozen, so she'd become incapable of either thought or action. Her hand tingled. 'I...I just need to find the light....'

she finally managed, stammering slightly. *Why* did Jason always reduce her to the gauchest kind of girl?

'It's here.' Jason reached past her and flicked on the switch. Emily took a hasty step back as the room was cast into unrelieved fluorescent light.

She felt a blush heat her cheeks, which made no sense because surely there was nothing to be embarrassed about. Yet she felt, strangely, as she had seven years ago, when she'd offered herself to him so innocently, only to be rejected.

And Jason was glaring at her again, just as he had then. Really, he looked quite cross. Emily felt a flicker of annoyance and the emotion relieved her. At least it was familiar. She took another step back. 'Thanks,' she said briskly, tucking her hair behind her ears. 'I suppose I'll see you around, if you're staying in London for a bit.'

'Most certainly.' Jason's face was expressionless yet his gaze was steady on hers, steady and unsettling. He really didn't know her any more, she reminded herself. She was completely different and far more experienced now than she'd been at seventeen. A bit more experienced, anyway. And hopefully a little less scatty.

'I'm sure you have things to do,' she said in that same brisk, brittle voice. 'And I must get home. Goodnight, Jason.' And without looking back, she hurried down the hall to the safety of her office, strangely and annoyingly disconcerted, almost as much as the seventeen-year-old who'd run from the ballroom in tears.

CHAPTER TWO

EMILY gazed at the woman seated across from her desk, noticed how her fingers nervously pleated the rather wrinkled fabric of her cheap black skirt, a cautious smile brightening her lovely features. Helen Smith was a beautiful young woman, a few years younger than Emily, with a cloud of dark hair like a soft halo around her pale face.

'So.' Emily smiled encouragingly as she scanned Helen's scanty CV. 'You worked as a waitress up in Liverpool…'

'And I temped for a while in an office,' Helen offered helpfully. Her voice was soft and lilting. 'I answered the telephones. Mr Kingsley thought I might do the same here. He said one of your receptionists was on maternity leave.'

Emily wondered—not for the first time—just what Jason's relationship to the lovely Helen Smith could possibly be. Did she have anything to do with this mysterious personal business? 'Yes, Sally just had a baby boy.' Emily returned the CV to her desk; there really wasn't much to see there. 'So Mr

Kinglsey is right,' she said with a smile. 'We have an opening.'

'He's a nice man,' Helen whispered, looking down at her lap. Her hair fell forward, obscuring her face, and Emily wondered if she'd ever seemed this young and…clueless. Probably. She felt a stab of sympathy for Helen Smith even as she glanced at her bitten, ragged nails and worn jumper. She could certainly use a manicure and a makeover.

Could it actually be possible that Jason was interested in Helen? She *was* beautiful, despite the nails and clothes, although Jason's dates had always been socialites or starlets. Still, he'd never taken them seriously. Maybe a woman like Helen Smith, lovely and fragile, would capture his heart. Why on earth did she care anyway? Annoyed, Emily turned back to Helen's scanty CV. 'He's a very nice employer,' she said firmly, and Helen nodded shyly.

'It was good of him to listen to Richard about me.'

Emily raised her eyebrows, curiosity sharpening inside her. 'Richard?'

Helen blushed, which made her look lovelier, her cheeks as pink as roses, her complexion like a china doll's. Emily had never doubted her own basic attractiveness, yet right now she was conscious of her rather round-cheeked, healthful appeal, a bit different from Helen's fragile loveliness. 'My…well, he's just my friend, I suppose. We grew up together, back in Liverpool, and…' Helen's blush deepened and she pulled the sleeves of her worn jumper down over her hands, just as Emily remembered doing as an angst-ridden teen. 'Well, I'm older now,' Helen continued hesitantly, 'and Richard thought if I moved to London, and we spent a bit more time together...' She trailed off, nibbling her lip. 'Richard said that perhaps—in time—we might make a go of it,' she finished almost apologetically.

'He said that?' Emily asked before she could stop herself. It sounded most unromantic.

Helen stared at her with wide grey eyes that reflected every emotion, including now a woeful uncertainty. 'Yes...you know, to see if we're a good fit.'

Like a pair of shoes. Emily suppressed a shudder. She could not imagine anything less appealing. Still, she was hardly one to judge. The two relationships she'd entered into in a spirit of cautious optimism had been, if not disasters, then surely disappointments. She most certainly wasn't looking for a third. Still, if you were going to have a relationship, surely you wanted something a bit more than what this Richard was offering.

'Sounds very sensible,' she said. Too sensible. Where was the romance? The *love*? There was nothing sensible about either, as far as she was concerned, although she had no first-hand experience. She'd never been in love, not even close, and she doubted it would ever happen. True love matches—like her own mother and father's—were rare, which was why

Emily had been happy to help Steph and Tim along. She'd just about given up finding it for herself. 'Does Richard work for Kingsley Engineering?' she asked, mentally going through the several hundred employees Jason had on his payroll. There were several Richards.

'Yes, he's worked on a project with Mr Kingsley in Africa,' Helen answered. 'He just got back.'

Emily nodded, for now she knew just who Helen's Richard was. Richard Marsden, one of a handful of Jason's protégés, a solid-looking engineer with an earnest expression, a nervous tic and absolutely no sense of humour. Of course he would suggest such a thing. She could just see him sitting Helen down on his sofa and outlining his five-year plan for their relationship, with accompanying PowerPoint presentation. It all sounded rather dreadful. 'Well,' she said diplomatically, 'it will certainly be nice for you to be able to spend some time with him.'

'Yes…' Helen sounded hesitant and, although Emily didn't blame her, she decided they'd had enough personal conversation. Part of her success in Human Resources was to know both when to employ and to curb the personal aspect of her position. 'Well, since Mr Kingsley can vouch for you, I'm certainly willing to hire you. We'll just fill out some forms and then I'll show you around the reception area.'

Helen beamed. 'Thank you, Miss Wood.'

'Please, call me Emily. We're all friendly here.'

Emily watched as Helen bent her dark head to fill out the forms, a sudden, gentle sort of protectiveness stealing over her. The girl really did seem terribly innocent. She would certainly need someone to look out for her, show her the ropes. And, more importantly, a bit of fun. Clearly Richard wasn't going to do it.

'Come on, then,' she said when Helen had finished the forms. 'We can grab a coffee before I show you 'round. You can meet a few people.' A few people other than Richard Marsden, she added silently.

The rest of her first day as Head of Human Resources passed uneventfully enough, with no more than the usual common complaints and banal paperwork to round out the hire of Helen that morning. She was surprised to find it already past five o'clock and most of her department gone when she finally finished her last email and pressed send.

'A successful first day, it seems.'

Emily looked up to see Jason standing in her doorway, and she wondered how she could have missed his approach. Her heart certainly gave a sudden, surprising lurch now.

'Jason, you startled me.' She smiled up at him, noticing the deeper grooves from his mouth to nose, the faint fanning of wrinkles at the corners of his eyes. The African sun had aged him a bit, but it was not unattractive. Jason could certainly carry off a rather dignified look. And he was quite a bit older…

he was nearing forty. Time to think of marrying, perhaps. The thought was unsettling, only because she could not imagine Jason with a wife. He would probably pick someone to suit him just like Richard was with Helen. She could just see him compiling some sort of list. *Must be handy with an iron, a golf club and a gardening spade....*

'Yes, it was successful,' she said, stressing the word lightly. 'No less than you'd expect, of course.'

'Of course.' He strolled into her office. He wore, as usual, a dark suit with a crisp shirt and blue silk tie, a woollen trench coat over one arm. He looked utterly put together and as always a little remote, and yet he seemed somehow different too. Or perhaps she was the one who was different, for she couldn't quite keep her gaze from roving over him as that citrusy scent of his aftershave assaulted her senses.

She rose from her desk, glad she'd chosen a cherry-red power suit with a fitted jacket and miniskirt for her first day as Head. Admittedly, her skirt was a *bit* on the short side, and she saw Jason's gaze flick to her bare legs before his mouth tightened into a faint but familiar line of disapproval.

Feeling a little impish, Emily held one foot out for him to examine. 'Oh, do you like my shoes?' she asked, widening her eyes innocently. Today she'd worn a pair of matching red stilettos with diamanté straps. She wasn't generally that into shoes, but these had been hard to resist. And they matched her suit perfectly.

Jason stared at her stretched-out leg, looking decidedly unimpressed. 'Very pretty,' he said after a moment. 'Although not necessarily work attire.'

'Well,' Emily told him, unable to resist the opportunity to bait him just a bit more, 'I had to liven up this suit somehow.'

For a split second Jason looked positively thunderous, and Emily wondered if he was actually angry. Then he glanced at her, smiling, his eyes lightening to the honey colour she'd seen last night, and he said, 'Trust me, Emily, your clothes do not need livening up. Now, how about a bite to eat and you can tell me all about your first day?'

Emily blinked in shock. She had been half-expecting Jason to check up on her since it was the first day of her new position, but this? 'Dinner?' she repeated rather stupidly, and Jason's smile widened.

'That is the idea. Usually, around six o'clock, people like to eat and drink. Sustenance, you know, as well as a social habit.'

Emily's mouth twitched in a smile. She'd forgotten about Jason's dry sense of humour. And, despite her surprise at the invitation, she realised she'd like to have dinner with him. She was curious about how he'd changed, and even what this personal business was. And there was something about Jason—something oddly different—that she wanted to understand. Or at least explore. 'Actually,

I'm famished,' she told him as she reached for her coat. 'I skipped lunch. So yes, you can treat me to dinner.'

Jason watched as Emily slid a form-fitting trench coat over her already clinging suit. It didn't even cover her legs. For a coat, it was remarkably revealing. He felt himself frown, already regretting his impulse invitation. He hadn't even meant to come down to Emily's office; he had plans that evening, and he'd meant to walk straight outside to his car. Yet somehow he'd taken this little detour, and once he'd seen Emily hold out one perfectly shaped golden leg, her eyes sparkling with laughter, his resolve had crumbled to dust.

He'd kept away from her for seven years; she was nearly twenty-five now. She was experienced, if the social pages were anything to go by, and surely a single evening—a little bit of light flirting—wouldn't harm anyone. It was just, Jason told himself, an itch he needed to scratch. It wouldn't go anywhere. It couldn't. He wouldn't even kiss her.

Yet already he was reaching for his BlackBerry, and he quickly sent a rather terse text to cancel the rest of his plans for the evening. He clicked the button on his keys to unlock the car, and Emily started in surprise.

'You own a Porsche?' she said, clearly surprised.

Jason opened her door, breathing in the strawberry scent of her hair and something else, something warm and feminine that had lust jolting through him yet again. *Just dinner.* 'It appears that I do,' he said, and she rolled her eyes as she slid into the sumptuous leather interior.

'Quite a nice ride. It's not what I'd expect at all.'

'Oh?' Jason slid into the driver's seat. 'I didn't know you had expectations about my mode of transport.'

'Yes, but that's it exactly, isn't it?' Emily said with a laugh. She shook her hair back over her shoulders in a golden waterfall. 'Your "mode of transport". I'd expect something basic and, well, boring for you, just a car to get you from point A to point B. Of course,' she teased, 'the colour is a bit dull. Navy-blue doesn't do it for me, I'm afraid.'

Jason stared at her for a second, utterly nonplussed by her rather brutal assessment of him. *Boring?* And he'd been thinking she still had a little crush on him. Well, that was him sorted. 'Boring,' he repeated musingly as he started the car. 'And dull. I wonder if I should be offended.'

'You can hardly be offended by that, Jason!'

Now he really *was* offended. Most women didn't think he was boring at all. Most women were eager to spend an evening with him. Yet here Emily sat sprawled in the seat across from him, her skirt riding up on her slim thighs, looking at him as if he were her doddering old uncle whom she had to humour.

Yet she hadn't looked at him like that last night. He still remembered the brief, enticing touch of her hand on his chest. She'd been startled by the electric current that had suddenly snapped between them; he knew she'd felt it. He certainly had. Now he slid her a sideways glance as he revved the engine, causing Emily to laugh a little as she instinctively grabbed the door handle. 'Can't I?' he murmured.

'Well, honestly,' she said once he'd pulled out of the office's underground car park and begun to drive down Euston Road at quite a sedate speed. 'You've always been—'

'Boring?' He heard the slight edge to his voice and strove to temper it. This was not how he'd pictured this evening starting.

'Well, not boring precisely,' Emily allowed. 'But… predictable. Cautious. Steady.' Jason kept his face expressionless although he felt his brows start to draw together in an instinctive glower. She was actually *patronising* him. 'You never took part in the games and scrapes we got into—'

'By "we" I assume you mean you, Isobel and Jack,' Jason returned dryly. At Emily's nod, he continued, 'You might do well to remember, Em, that you're twelve years younger than I am. While you were getting into these so-called scrapes, I was in university.' His hands tightened on the wheel as the difference in their ages struck its necessary blow. Emily might be twenty-five, but she was still young. And in many ways, naive. Innocent, if not utterly, not to mention scatty, silly and far too frivolous.

She was entirely wrong for him. Wrong for what he wanted.

Wrong for a wife.

'Well, of course I know that,' she said. 'But, even so…you've always been a bit *disapproving*, Jason. Even of Jack—'

'You didn't have to live with him,' Jason returned, keeping his voice mild. Of course everyone loved Jack. Jack was *fun*, except when it was Jason fetching him from boarding school after he'd been expelled, or from a party where he'd passed out. Fortunately, Jack had settled down since he'd been married, but Jason still remembered his younger brother's turbulent teen years. He'd helped him out because their father never would, and Jack had no memories of their mother. He had precious few himself…and the ones he did, he'd sometimes rather forget.

'Still,' Emily persisted in that same teasing tone, 'I remember the lectures you gave me. When I picked a few flowers from your garden, you positively *glowered*. You terrified me—'

'By a few flowers you mean all the daffodils.' They had been his mother's favourite, and he'd been furious with her for beheading them all, as he remembered.

'Was it all of them?' Her eyebrows arched in surprise. 'Oh, dear. I was a bit of a brat, wasn't I?'

'I didn't want to be the one to say it,' Jason murmured, and was rewarded with a gurgle of throaty laughter that made him feel as if he'd just stuck his finger in an electric socket. His whole body felt wired, alive and pulsating with pure lust. This evening really had been a mistake. He was playing with fire, and while he could handle a few burns, Emily surely couldn't. That was why he'd always stayed away, and why he should keep at it. Right now he could have been sitting down to dinner with Patience Felton-Smythe, a boring woman with a horsey face who liked to garden and knit and was on the board of three charities. In short, the kind of woman he intended to marry.

Emily gazed out of the window at the blur of traffic, the streets of London slick with rain. Although it was only the beginning of November, the Christmas lights had already been strung along Regent Street and their lights were streakily reflected on the pavement below.

'Where are we going?' she asked as Jason turned onto Brook Street.

'Claridge's,' he said and Emily let out a little laugh.

'I should have known. Somewhere upscale and respectable and just a little bit stodgy.'

'Like me?' Jason filled in as they pulled up to the landmark hotel.

Emily smiled sweetly. She *had* offended Jason with her offhand remark. 'You said it, not me.'

'You didn't need to. But, in any case, Claridge's has had a bit of a remake over the years. You might find it's the same with me.' He tossed the keys to the valet and came around to help Emily out of the car, his hand strong and firm as he guided her from the low-slung Porsche—not easy to manage in her stiletto heels and short skirt—and continued to hold her hand as he led her into the restaurant. Emily didn't protest, although she surely should have. There was something comforting and really rather nice about the way his fingers threaded through hers, his grip sure and strong.

It reminded her of when she'd been younger, and no matter what she'd done or where she'd gone, she'd trusted implicitly that Jason would be there to save her. Scold her too, undoubtedly, but she'd always known with him she was safe.

Yet as Jason glanced back at her, his eyes glinting, turning them the colour of dark honey, she had to acknowledge that something about holding Jason's hand didn't feel like when she was younger at all. In fact it felt quite different—different enough for a strange new uneasiness to ripple through her, and she smiled and slipped her hand from his as the maître d' led them to a secluded table in a corner of the iconic restaurant.

'So what's the occasion, exactly?' Emily asked as she opened the menu and began to peruse its offerings.

'Occasion?'

'I can't think the last time you took me out to dinner, if ever.'

Jason's lips twitched. 'There's a first time for everything.'

'I suppose, but...' Emily paused, cocking her head as she gazed at Jason; his hair was a little damp and rumpled from the rain and he had an endearingly studious expression on his face as he perused the wine list. She could see the faint shadow of stubble on his jaw, and it made him look surprisingly attractive. Sexy, even, which was ridiculous because she'd never thought of Jason that way—

Except for that once, and that was *not* going to be repeated.

'Are you checking up on me?' she asked, and Jason glanced up from the wine list.

'Checking up on you? You sound like you have a guilty conscience, Em. Too many parties?'

'No, it's just...' She paused, uncertain how to articulate how odd it was to be here with Jason, almost as if they were on a date. Which was ridiculous, because she knew Jason didn't think of her that way—hadn't he proved it on the dance floor seven years ago? Emily was quite sure nothing had changed there.

Except *she* had changed, of course. She'd grown up and moved long past that silly moment of infatuation with staid, stuffy Jason. And while she was perfectly happy to have dinner with an old family friend, she wasn't sure she wanted some kind of lecture. Had her father asked Jason to keep an eye on her, now he was back in London for a fair bit? It was quite possible.

'Just no lectures,' she said, wagging a finger at him, and Jason shook his head.

'I think you're a little too old for lectures, Em. Unless you misbehave, of course.' There was something almost wicked about Jason's smile, his eyes glinting in the candlelit dimness of the room, and Emily felt her stomach dip again. He turned back to the menu and she decided she must have imagined that suggestive undercurrent, that little glimpse of wickedness. There was nothing wicked about Jason Kingsley at all. He was the most law-abiding citizen she had ever known.

'I promise not to,' she replied, tossing her hair, and Jason beckoned the waiter over to the table to take their orders.

Emily ordered and then glanced around the room as Jason ordered for himself, a low murmur she didn't really hear. Most of the diners were businessmen making deals, or well-heeled pensioners. This place really was a little stodgy.

'The chicken? Adventurous, Em,' Jason said, slanting her an amused look as the waiter left.

Emily gave him her own flippant look right back. She'd been a notoriously picky eater as a child, as Jason undoubtedly remembered. 'The braised calf livers aren't to my taste.'

'Still picky?'

'Discriminating is the word I'd use. And not as

much as you might remember, Jason. I have changed, you know.'

'I don't doubt it.' He paused, his long, supple fingers toying with the stem of his water glass. 'I suppose,' he said musingly, 'there's quite a bit I don't know about you now. I've been gone, most of the time at least, for so long.'

'But now you're back to stay?'

He shrugged. 'For as long as needed.'

Emily nodded in understanding. 'On this personal business of yours?'

A frown creased his brow before his expression cleared and he flashed her a quick, knowing smile. 'Yes.'

She couldn't help but laugh; he wouldn't give anything away. He never did, but then she'd never thought Jason had any secrets before. Or at least secrets worth knowing. 'You're a man of mystery now, aren't you?'

'Rather than boring?' Jason filled in, one eyebrow arched.

'I think I hurt your feelings when I said that.'

'Only a little bit. As retribution, I told the waiter to bring you the calf livers rather than the chicken.'

Her eyes widened as she realised she actually hadn't heard what he'd ordered. 'You did not!'

'No, I didn't. But you believed me, didn't you?' His faint smile, for a second, formed into a fully fledged grin, and the effect of that smile had Emily unsettled yet again. She'd forgotten how white Jason's teeth were, how the dimple in his cheek deepened.... He really was a handsome man, which was, of course, what had compelled her to flirt with him seven years ago. She would not make the same mistake again.

'Only because you've always told me the truth, no matter how ungracious it is.'

He cocked his head, his gaze sweeping over her in considering assessment. 'Would you rather I lied?'

Emily thought of times Jason had told her the unvarnished truth when no one else would: when she was fourteen, she'd had a terrible spot on the tip of her nose. She'd been horribly embarrassed, and in a moment of desperation she'd asked Jason if he'd noticed it.

Straight-faced, he'd said, *Em, how could I not? But I still like you, spots and all.*

And when she'd been fifteen and missing her mother, who'd died when she was only three, she'd asked him if one ever stopped missing one's mum. She'd never met his mother; she'd died when he was eight years old.

No, he said, *you never stop. But it does get easier. Sometimes.*

His words had comforted her because she'd known them for truth rather than mere sentiment.

'No,' she said now, with her own surprised honesty, 'I wouldn't rather you lied. I suppose you need someone in your life who will tell you the truth.'

'I'll always do that.' His gaze lingered on her for

a moment longer than she expected, so a sudden warmth spread through her limbs, a new unsettling awareness that she could hardly credit. This was *Jason*. She felt a rush of relief when the sommelier came with the wine and Emily watched as Jason, with that same easy assurance, swilled it in his glass before taking a sip and then nodding his approval. When the man had left, he raised his glass, the deep ruby-red of the wine catching the candlelight, in a toast.

'To old friends and new beginnings,' he said, his gaze still lingering, Emily raised her own glass, as well.

'Hear, hear.'

'So,' Jason said once they had each taken a sip of wine, 'how is Helen getting on?'

'Ah, I knew there was an ulterior motive to this dinner.'

'Not at all,' Jason replied blandly. 'But, since you interviewed her this morning, I thought I might as well ask.'

'Well, I hired her as you asked me to. I think she'll do well enough. She hardly has the experience, though.'

'I didn't expect her to.'

Emily raised her eyebrows. 'A charity case?'

'Just a kindness,' Jason replied mildly.

Emily reached for her wine again, suppressing a sharp stab—of something. Whatever uncomfortable emotion was assailing her was not one she wanted to name. 'She's quite beautiful, you know.'

'Actually, I don't. As you might recall, I told you yesterday that I'd never met her.'

'Ah, yes.' Emily pursed her lips. 'I do recall now. You wanted to hire her as a favour to Richard Marsden.'

Jason cocked his head. 'I don't think I mentioned him by name, but yes.'

'Because,' Emily continued wryly, but with a little bite to her words, 'Helen and Richard are going to make a *go* of it.'

Jason paused, his wine glass halfway to his lips. 'You sound as if you don't approve.'

'Who am I to approve or disapprove?' Emily replied, her eyebrows arching innocently.

'It sounds eminently sensible to me,' Jason said with a brisk reasonableness Emily didn't like.

'Oh, yes, very sensible,' she agreed. 'Hardly romantic, though.'

'Romantic?' Jason frowned. 'Is it meant to be romantic?'

He sounded so nonplussed that Emily almost wanted to laugh, yet something in her—some deep, hidden well of emotion—kept her from amusement. Instead, she almost felt hurt, which made no sense at all and so she pushed the thought away. 'Well, in general, Jason,' she said, as if explaining basic arithmetic to a slightly backward child, 'the kind of relationship Helen was talking about with Richard is meant to be romantic rather than *sensible*. You're hardly choosing a…a pair of shoes when it comes to a girlfriend or even a wife—'

'I'm a great believer in sensible shoes.'

Emily narrowed her eyes, unable to tell whether Jason was joking or not. She had a feeling he wasn't. 'A girl likes to be swept a little bit off her feet, you know.'

'It sounds dangerous,' Jason replied, straight-faced. 'If you're swept off your feet, you could lose your balance. You might even fall.'

'Exactly,' Emily replied. 'You might fall in love, which is the whole point, isn't it? Rather than making a go of it.'

He eyed her thoughtfully. 'You seem to have taken exception to that expression.'

'I have,' Emily agreed with a bit more passion than she would have preferred to show. The glass of wine must be going to her head; she'd had hardly anything to eat since breakfast. 'I'd much rather stay single my whole life than be with someone who asks me to make a *go* of it,' she finished, her voice still sounding a little too loud.

'Duly noted. And are you planning to stay single, then?'

'As a matter of fact, yes,' she said, glad to see surprise flash across his features. 'I've no reason to get married.'

'No reason?'

'I'm not lonely or unhappy or dying to have

children,' Emily replied with a shrug and a bit more conviction than she actually felt. She didn't want to admit to Jason that she had no reason to get married because she hadn't met anyone worth marrying. Worth taking that risk for. 'I'm not going to wait around for Prince Charming to come and rescue me,' she declared, her tone starting to sound strident. Jason raised his eyebrows, a small smile playing about his mouth, clearly amused. 'I want to have fun.'

'Now that I can believe.'

She made a face at him. 'What's wrong with that? There's plenty of time to settle down.'

'For you, perhaps.'

'Oh, yes, I forget how old you are. One foot in the grave already.' She smiled at him, determined to stay light and teasing although for some reason she was feeling less and less so. 'In any case,' she said dismissively, 'I have friends, a job I love, a niece and nephew to cuddle and a man who adores me.'

Jason stilled. 'A man who adores you?' he queried in a tone of polite interest.

Emily couldn't help but laugh at Jason's suspicious look. He looked as though he thought she had some sort of toyboy on retainer. 'My father, of course.' She eyed him mischievously. 'Did you think I was talking about someone else?'

'I wondered,' he admitted blandly. 'But since you've been wittering on about your determination to stay single, I had to assume we were not talking about a romantic interest.'

'I wasn't wittering,' Emily said with some affront, and Jason raised his eyebrows.

'I apologise. You were waxing poetically.'

She made a face. 'That sounds worse.' To her surprise, she found she was enjoying this little repartee. She leaned forward, a sudden, sharp curiosity making her ask, 'And what about you, Jason? Any plans to be swept off your feet?'

His mouth quirked upwards, revealing that dimple. 'I thought I was meant to do the sweeping.'

Emily laughcd ruefully in acknowledgement. 'It sounds as if we're talking about cleaning a house. Do you intend to marry? Fall in love?' She'd spoken lightly, yet the question suddenly felt invasive, intimate, and she half-regretted asking it even though she wanted to know the answer. Badly.

Jason rotated his wine glass between his strong brown fingers; the simple action was strangely mesmerising. 'One does not necessarily require the other,' he finally said, and Emily felt a bizarre flicker of disappointment.

'And which would you prefer?' she asked, keeping her tone light and teasing. 'Love without marriage, or marriage without love?'

Jason took a sip of wine, his eyes meeting hers over the rim of the glass, his gaze now flat and forbidding. 'Love, in my opinion, is overrated.'

'A rather cynical point of view,' Emily returned

after a moment. She felt that flicker of disappointment again, and suppressed it. What did it matter what Jason thought of either love or marriage? 'What made you decide that?'

He lifted one shoulder in a shrug. 'Experience, I suppose. Anyone can say they love someone. It's just a bunch of words you can choose to believe or not. They don't make much difference, in the end.' He lapsed into a sudden silence, frowning, as if his own words had triggered an unpleasant thought— or memory. Then his expression cleared, as if by force of will, and he glanced up at her, smiling. 'Much better, in my opinion, to marry and, yes, even make a go of it than witter on about love—or wax poetically, as the case may be.' His eyes glinted with knowing humour, and Emily conceded the point with a little laugh although she wondered just what experience had made Jason so cynical...and what had made him frown quite like that.

'Be that as it may,' she said, 'a little poetry surely can't go amiss.'

'Yet you've written off both marriage and love, it would seem?'

Written off seemed a bit strong, but Emily didn't intend to debate the point. As far as Jason was concerned, written off would do very well indeed. 'I told you, I'm happy as I am.'

'Happy to have fun.'

'Yes.' She stared at him defiantly. He made fun sound like a naughty word. She knew he thought she was a bit scatty, perhaps even a little wild, and she took a perverse pleasure in confirming his opinion. Even if she still felt that bizarre flicker of hurt.

'Yet you seem to be interested in finding love and marriage for others,' Jason noted dryly. 'Stephanie and Tim being a case in point.'

'Just because I don't want it for me doesn't mean it isn't right for other people,' Emily replied breezily. 'I'm a great believer in love. Just not for myself. Not now, anyway.' She took a sip of wine, averting her eyes. She wasn't quite telling Jason the truth, but she had no intention of admitting that she wasn't looking for love because she didn't want to be disappointed when it proved impossible to find, or didn't live up to her expectations. She'd witnessed a love match first-hand—or almost. Even though her mother had died before she had any real memories of her, Emily had heard plenty of stories about Elizabeth Wood; she knew from her father—and his grief—that they had loved each other deeply and forever.

That kind of love didn't come to everyone. She was afraid it would never come to her. And it was much easier to convince herself—and Jason—that she'd never wanted it in the first place. 'In any case,' she continued in an effort to steer the conversation away from such personal matters, 'we were talking about Richard and Helen. And I think it's safe to say that I know a bit more about these things than you do.'

'These things?'

'What women want when it comes to romance. Love, even. I may not be looking for it myself, but that doesn't mean I don't know what most women want.' She'd had enough late-night sessions with friends over a bottle of wine or even just the idle chatter by the coffee machine at work to be quite the expert.

'Is that right?' He sounded amused, which annoyed her. She did, in fact, know what she was talking about, much more than Jason ever would. She could just imagine Jason sitting some poor woman down and asking her to make a go of it just like Richard Marsden had. Knowing Jason, he wouldn't ask; he'd insist. He'd probably propose marriage with a drawn-up business contract in his breast pocket. The thought sent an unreasonable flame of indignation burning through her.

'Yes, I do,' she told him firmly. 'Women want a man who will romance them, Jason. Woo them with flowers and compliments and thoughtfulness and… and lots of other things,' she finished a bit lamely. The wine was really going to her head; her brain felt rather fuzzy. 'And what they *don't* want is to have someone sit them down and tell them they *might* be suitable, but first they need a trial period.'

'I doubt Marsden said it like that.'

'Close enough. The meaning was clear.'

Jason cocked his head. 'And you don't think Helen Smith could tell Marsden just where to put it if she didn't like his idea?'

Emily let out a reluctant laugh. 'Perhaps—if she had more backbone. She's young and impressionable. In any case, another man will surely come and sweep her off her feet while Richard is deciding whether they can make a go of it or not. She's very beautiful.'

'So you've told me.' His mouth curved upwards once more. 'But if you ask me, which I am quite aware you are not, Richard's suggestion is very sensible. And, in the long run, far more romantic than a bunch of plastic-wrapped bouquets and meaningless compliments. I think he could be just the thing for her.'

'You make it sound as if Helen has a head cold and Richard is a couple of paracetamol,' Emily protested, her mind spinning in indignation over Jason's dismissal of everything she'd just said. Plastic-wrapped bouquets and meaningless compliments! God help the poor woman he decided to approach with his own sensible plan. 'That's not what a woman wants out of love or marriage, Jason.'

Jason leaned forward, his eyes alight. They really turned the most amazing colour sometimes, Emily thought a bit dazedly. Almost amber. She swallowed, aware that she probably shouldn't have had a second glass of wine. And where was their food?

'But you said you weren't interested in love or marriage,' he reminded her softly.

Emily swallowed again. Her throat felt very dry.

How had this conversation become so personal and… and *intimate*? 'I told you, I'm happy as I am.'

'With no intention of ever falling in love?'

With no intention of telling Jason any more about her own love life, or lack thereof, Emily amended silently. 'Perhaps love *is* overrated,' she said, throwing his own words back at him. 'I've had two relationships and although I didn't love either of the men involved, they were still definite disappointments. I'm not interested in searching for something that might never actually happen or even exist.' Or being hurt when it couldn't be found or didn't work out. She thought of her father's two decades of mourning. No, love wasn't overrated. But the aftermath might be underestimated.

Jason sat back, seemingly satisfied. 'Wise words. I quite agree.'

'So no love or marriage for you?' Emily said, meaning to tease, yet the question came out a little too serious.

'I didn't say that,' Jason said, and his dark gaze settled on Emily with a frown. 'I'll have to marry some time. I need an heir for Weldon, after all.'

Now *that* sounded positively medieval. She could see Jason arranging some awful marriage with a sour-faced socialite just because she was of good breeding stock. She shuddered. 'How practical of you,' she told him. 'I hope I'm not on your list of candidates.'

Jason's expression darkened, his brows snapping

together rather ferociously. 'Never fear, Em. You most certainly are not in the running.'

Well, he didn't have to sound *quite* so certain, Emily thought, feeling rather miffed by his hasty assurance. Of course they'd make a terrible couple—they were far too different—but did he really have to look as if the thought of marrying her was utterly repellent?

'Well, that's a relief, then,' she said lightly. 'So what kind of woman are you looking for?'

'Someone who shares my view on love and marriage.'

'Someone sensible, then.'

'Exactly.'

Emily made a face. It all sounded really rather horrible. 'Not one of the starlets or models you've usually had on your arm?' she said, trying to tease even though she still felt a bit miffed, and perhaps even hurt.

Jason frowned. 'Those were just dates,' he said. 'Not wife material.'

Emily shuddered theatrically. He sounded as if he were talking about a lump of clay, moulded to the shape he preferred. 'Well, good luck with that,' she said, her voice sharpening despite her intention to still sound so insouciant.

Jason inclined his head in acknowledgement. 'Thank you.'

Emily smiled back, but inside she found she really didn't like thinking about Jason and his sensible bride-to-be—whoever she was—at all.

CHAPTER THREE

THE rest of the meal passed pleasantly, and Emily was relieved to have the conversation move on to more innocuous matters. The chicken, although unadventurous, was delicious, and Emily found she enjoyed chatting with Jason about things as seemingly insignificant as the weather or the latest film. She'd forgotten what a dry sense of humour he had, so sometimes it took her a few seconds even to realise he was joking.

'Will you miss travelling?' she asked as the waiter cleared their plates. 'Since you're planning to be in London for a time.'

'I'll have other things to occupy me,' Jason replied easily.

Emily pursed her lips. 'This personal business.'

'You're quite curious about that.'

'Only because I can't imagine what it is. You've always been such an open book, Jason. No secrets. No surprises.'

Jason drummed his fingers on the table. He had rather nice fingers, Emily thought distractedly. Long and tapered. She'd been noticing them all evening. 'Boring again.'

'I really did insult you with that!' She laughed as Jason pulled a face.

'I never realised you thought me so stodgy,' he replied as he poured her another glass of wine.

'I shouldn't drink that,' she protested. 'I'm already feeling a bit tipsy.' Tipsy enough to have admitted it, as well.

Jason's lips curved in a knowing smile. 'And I recall that you say some quite interesting things when you've had a glass or two too many.'

Emily felt herself flush, for she knew just what Jason was referring to. *You're quite handsome, you know. Perhaps you'd like to kiss me.* Yet again he'd referenced that evening, that single dance when, buoyed by champagne and her own youthful naivety, she'd offered herself to him. Why did he keep mentioning it? Did he think it some great joke?

'Don't,' she said, trying to still sound light and teasing, and yet not quite pulling it off. She found she couldn't pretend it was all a joke, as she had the other day. Somehow, in the quiet candlelight, with Jason holding her gaze over the table, she couldn't summon that light, airy insouciance that she always covered herself with, almost like armour. 'I'm a bit sensitive about that,' she managed lightly and Jason sat back, his expression turning speculative.

'Why?'

Emily choked back a startled laugh. 'Because you humiliated me, that's why!'

Jason stared at her, his expression so utterly nonplussed that once again Emily was torn between laughter and a strange sense of hurt. 'I humiliated you?' he repeated, his tone quietly incredulous. 'Sorry, Em, but I don't quite see how that happened.'

She shook her head, refusing to discuss it. They'd gone over it once already, and it really was time to relegate that episode to the dim and dusty past. 'Never mind. It hardly matters, Jason. It was seven years ago. I was practically a child.'

'I know,' he said, so softly Emily almost didn't hear him. 'I was quite aware of that at the time.'

Discomfited again, Emily said, 'In any case, we were talking about Helen and Richard.'

'Is there more to say on that subject?'

'You might not think so, but as someone newly arrived to London, Helen surely would like to experience all it has to offer and meet a few—'

'Oh, no, you don't, Emily.' Jason put his glass down and looked at her with a certain knowing sharpness that Emily didn't really like, but at least she recognised it. This was how Jason had always looked at her, how he *was*, and it almost relieved her to have him treating her the same as he always did. Then she could treat him as she always did, and she'd stop feeling so unsettled, so…restless. 'You aren't planning to organise Helen, are you?'

'Organise?' Emily repeated, widening her eyes.

'Yes, just as you did with Stephanie. She might have been your work superior and several years older than you, but you had her well in hand within months.'

Emily stared at him in surprise and with a little bit of affront. He made her sound like a bossy know-it-all when she was just *outgoing*. Unlike some people. 'How would you know?' she demanded. 'If I remember correctly, you'd swanned off to Asia at the time.'

'Swanned off?' Jason repeated in wry disbelief. 'I don't think working twelve hours a day on a flood retention basin in Burma involved any swanning.'

'How would you know what I was up to?'

Jason shrugged, his face impassive. 'I have my sources. I know you organised her on a round of dinner parties and drinks outings, and Tim wasn't your first attempt at a blind date—'

Emily's mouth dropped open most inelegantly. 'You've been *spying* on me—'

'Keeping tabs,' Jason cut across her. 'I hired you when you came to London, and of course I had a vested interest in making sure you were keeping safe. Especially considering your father, Isobel and Jack would all have my head if anything happened to you.'

'Nothing did,' Emily said a bit sulkily. She didn't like the thought of Jason knowing what she was up to. Here she'd been thinking to show him how sophisticated and poised she'd become in the last few years, only to discover he'd been keeping an eye on her all along, as if she were some recalcitrant child.

'In any case,' Jason continued, 'my point is that while I'm perfectly happy for you to welcome Helen into the company and even show her around a bit, I draw the line at having her *meet* people or, God help us, involving yourself in any more matchmaking.'

'So you do admit I had something to do with Steph and Tim!' Emily said in triumph, and Jason reached for his wine.

'Undoubtedly, but I'd like you to leave Helen and Richard alone so they *can* make a go of it, if they so choose.'

Emily sighed, rolling her eyes for dramatic effect. 'Very well. It is quite clear to me that you do not have a romantic bone in your body.'

'On the contrary,' Jason replied equably, 'I think it shows a remarkable sensitivity on my part, that I concern myself with them at all.' He smiled blandly. 'You, however, need not concern yourself.'

'As Head of Human Resources, it's my responsibility to make sure Helen settles in—'

'I'm sure Richard has that well in hand.'

'Ha!' Emily shook her head. 'He probably thinks inviting Helen over for some television and takeaway is enough.'

Jason narrowed his eyes. 'You really do have something against him, don't you?'

'No—' Emily protested, but Jason cut across her.

'Or is it just more amusing—and easier—to involve yourself in other people's lives rather than consider your own?'

Emily blinked; the banter had suddenly turned a bit too personal. His accusation hurt. 'Are you saying I'm a busybody?'

'I'm giving it to you straight,' Jason corrected, a small smile barely softening his words. 'Don't meddle.' He signalled for the waiter. 'And now I think I should take you home.'

Emily was irritatingly aware that Jason had just ended their conversation whether she had something more to say or not. So typical of him, and even though she'd fully intended to show him just how sophisticated and poised she'd become, she still felt like a scolded child in his presence, complete with braces and plaits. She rose from the table as gracefully as she could, well aware that although she wasn't drunk, she was definitely operating with a little buzz.

'Thank you for dinner.'

'The pleasure was all mine.' Jason's lips twitched as he gazed at her; Emily knew she probably looked a little sulky. 'Literally,' he added.

She felt compelled to say, 'I don't meddle.'

'And I'm not boring,' Jason whispered, his breath fanning her ear, his hand on the small of her back as he guided her from the restaurant. 'It seems we have to get to know each other all over again, Em.'

Before Emily could think of a reply, or even untangle just what Jason might have meant, the valet was fetching his Porsche and she was sliding into the leather interior, her head resting against the seat as the world spun dizzily around her. Definitely too much wine.

'Poor, Em,' Jason murmured as he pulled away from the kerb. 'Did you have anything to eat today?'

'A few crackers at lunch,' Emily said with a sigh. 'I'm a notorious lightweight, but even this is a bit much for me.' She felt her stomach lurch and grimaced.

'I hope,' Jason said, 'you're not going to be sick all over my car.'

Emily tried to laugh, although the idea was alarmingly possible. 'If I am,' she said, 'it's because the chicken was off, not because I drank too much.'

Jason laughed softly. 'Perhaps you should have tried the calf livers.' He reached over and laid a cool hand on her forehead, his fingers massaging her temples with deft lightness. She inhaled the citrusy tang of his aftershave, felt the graze of his thumb on her cheekbone. The touch managed to both soothe and stimulate her, which made her body feel even more confused. Jason had never touched her like this before; he'd never really touched her at all. 'Maybe you should close your eyes,' he suggested.

Emily obeyed, her head resting against the seat as she took a few deep breaths and her stomach finally settled itself. Jason left his hand on her forehead, the pressure cool and comforting. Emily had the bizarre desire to put her hand over his own, to keep his palm there, pressed against her. 'Sorry,' she said after a moment, and then added, compelled to honesty, 'And here I wanted to show you how sophisticated I am.'

'Sophisticated?' Belatedly, Emily realised she probably shouldn't have said that. 'Sophistication is overrated, Em.'

'Like love?' The words slipped out of their own accord. She felt as much as heard Jason's hesitation.

'Yes,' he finally said, removing his hand, and she opened her eyes. Jason had stopped the car, and she saw they were in front of her building. The car suddenly seemed very small and dark and quiet, the only sound their breathing.

Emily curled her fingers around the door handle. 'Well, goodnight, then,' she said, her voice a whisper in the dark, and Jason reached for his own door.

'I'll see you home.'

Emily fumbled in her bag for her keys, conscious of Jason next to her, looming like a dark shadow. She lived in a block of mansion flats, with separate keys for the front door as well as the door to her own flat. Now, in her befuddlement, she shoved the wrong key into the door, jamming it uselessly.

'Here, let me,' Jason said, and his fingers wrapped around hers as he took the key from her and replaced it with the other, then turned the lock easily and opened the door.

The elegant little foyer was lit only by a small table lamp and in the shadowy light Emily could see Jason's expression, his gaze solemn and yet somehow intent in a way that unnerved her. This whole evening had unnerved her because even though Jason had, for the most part, acted exactly as she expected him to, authoritative and a little annoying and yet still affectionately, impossibly Jason, he'd been different too. The whole evening had been different and, at this moment, with Jason still gazing at her in that intent, *intense* way, Emily could not articulate even to herself why. She couldn't think at all.

'You don't have to come upstairs,' she said, and then blushed at what sounded like some kind of ridiculous innuendo. 'I'm fine—'

'I'll leave you to it, then,' Jason said and, after a second's pause where they simply stared at each other, he lifted his hand, his fingers suspended in air, a whisper away from her face. Emily held her breath, unsure of what he intended or why she felt a strange swooping sensation in her stomach, as if she'd missed a step, or the floor had fallen away completely. Then Jason let his fingers brush her cheek, no more than a whisper of a touch, his fingertips barely trailing her jaw as a smile softened his features. Yet before Emily could even process it or the feel of his fingers on her skin, his expression hardened once more, his brows snapping together as he dropped his hand. 'Goodnight, Em,' he said, and then he was gone.

Emily sagged against the stairs, her mind spinning more than ever before, and this time it had nothing to do with the wine.

Jason slid back into his Porsche, cursing himself for almost kissing her. Or maybe for not kissing her. His body and mind were clearly at war, both seething with unfulfilled desire. This evening had been incredibly enjoyable, and therefore a big mistake. Why was he wasting his time with Emily? It so clearly couldn't go anywhere. He wouldn't let it.

And yet still here he was, wanting to be with her because it was so intensely pleasurable to listen to her banter, to hear her throaty laugh, to watch the lamplight pick out the golden glints in her hair. He'd felt vibrantly and vividly alive in her presence, and when she drew close to him he couldn't keep himself from touching her. Her skin had felt like warm silk.

This time Jason cursed aloud. This was *Emily*. Emily Wood, his nearest neighbour, his sister-in-law, the girl whose plaits he'd tugged and tears he'd wiped. She was a woman now, yes, but she was also scatty and silly and a little bit wild, and a completely inappropriate choice for a wife. As for anything else…that was, if not unimaginable, then impossible.

He could not have a cheap affair or easy fling with Emily Wood. He thought of all the reasons why being with her was a bad, bad idea: their families were related; she was young, more naive than she'd like him to believe; and most importantly, most disastrously, she had ideas about love. Romance. She might not be looking for love or marriage now, but *convenient* and *sensible* were clearly not in her vocabulary. He'd seen the stars in her eyes.

Just as he'd seen the stars in his mother's eyes wink slowly out. He'd lived with the resulting darkness, and it made him all the more determined to find the kind of wife his father should have had, the kind of wife he needed: convenient, sensible, practical. No romance. No love. No Emily.

Yet still the thought of her slid into his mind with a slyly seductive whisper and he found he could picture having an affair with Emily Wood all too easily. He could quite vividly imagine the silken slide of her lips against his, the heavy weight of her hair under his hand. And more…much more than that. Her body fitted close to his, her legs entwined with his…

Jason called a halt to that line of thinking, pleasurable as it was. No matter what her age now, Emily was still off-limits. He'd told her the truth when he'd said she was not on his list of candidates for a wife. He'd returned to London on *very* personal business, and that was the matter of finding someone to marry. He was thirty-seven years old and his father's health had begun to fail. He needed an heir. Emily might think that was awful and archaic, but Jason preferred to see it as practical.

Practical and without the kind of emotional expectations that had made his own mother miserable, and his father a widower. Love wasn't just overrated, it was inadvisable. Fraught with disappointment and danger, which was why Jason chose to avoid it altogether…as would his wife. No meaningless words, useless gestures, nameless disappointments. Just mutual respect and affection, the most solid basis for a lasting union.

What was not practical was envisioning Emily Wood in that role. Scatty, silly, teasing and tempting Emily Wood. Spoiled darling of the social pages, not to mention her father. Looking for love, even if she didn't realise it. Hell, she was arranging it for other people.

She was not remotely suitable to be his convenient, carefully chosen wife.

And she thought he was boring.

He laughed aloud, the sound rueful, as he acknowledged just how much Emily's careless remark had annoyed him. He really had thought she was still a little besotted with him, and the fact that she wasn't made him realise the extent of his own foolish arrogance. Although she hadn't thought he was boring when he'd touched her. He'd heard that slight indrawn breath, felt the crackle between them. Emily had definitely not been bored then.

And he'd barely been able to keep himself from cupping her face and drawing those lush lips towards his for the kiss he'd long denied himself.

And would continue denying himself, even if he longed to prove to Emily just how *exciting* he could be. He was in the business of finding a wife, not a lover. And despite the lust that still fired his body, he knew Emily could never be either.

CHAPTER FOUR

EMILY woke up with a vicious headache, which did not endear her to anyone, including Jason. She still had a vague sense of unease from their dinner last night, although she could not articulate why. It had been kind of Jason to take her out and, since she could be a bit more rational about things in the cold light of morning, she was honest enough to acknowledge that it was perfectly right and fair for Jason to be checking up on her. She'd expected it, years ago, and had been surprised and even a little hurt when he'd left so abruptly after he'd hired her. So why should it bother her now?

That part of their conversation, Emily acknowledged, didn't bother her. No, it was the other, hidden part, the way his eyes had glinted so knowingly and his mouth had quirked up at the corners and he'd murmured in that low hum of a voice that made her feel as if she wasn't with Jason at all, at least not the Jason she knew and depended on and sometimes—often—was irritated with, the Jason who teased and scolded and kept her in line. She was with a different

Jason, someone she wondered whether she knew at all.

It was most unsettling.

Emily pushed *that* Jason out of her mind as she hurried to dress for work. Her headache had made her slow and after popping a few paracetamol she quickly dressed, grabbed her bag and hurried out of her flat.

She was looking forward to seeing Helen again, who was reporting to HR to start her first day at nine o'clock sharp. Helen was already waiting when Emily arrived, wincing slightly at the bright office light, at five minutes after nine.

'Sorry…a bit of a slow morning.'

'Oh, it's all right,' Helen said quickly. 'It's just so good to be here.' She smiled, a faint blush tinging her cheeks. 'I am a bit nervous, though,' she admitted.

'I'm sure you'll be fine,' Emily assured her as she put her things away and reached for Helen's paperwork. 'Come on then, let's get you sorted.'

Fifteen minutes later, Helen was seated comfortably at the front reception area, with Jane, the other, more senior receptionist, showing her how to work the bank of blinking telephones. There had been a push a few years ago to move to a more modern automated system of taking calls, but Jason had refused, and Emily could guess why. Two receptionists would be out of jobs. Besides, she supposed he was a bit old-fashioned that way, and the personal touch of a real human voice on the other end of the line was always appreciated. It was one of the many things that made Kingsley Engineering head and shoulders above other engineering firms, and Jason Kingsley a wealthy man.

Now Emily watched as Helen's eyes rounded at the seemingly complicated system of buttons and switches, her expression glazing over as Jane explained how to hold a call while answering another one, and then reeled off a list of employees who never liked to take calls, and other ones who preferred to be interrupted.

'Goodness,' Helen murmured. She'd been writing down what Jane was saying, but had abandoned the effort mid-list and simply stared around her in what looked to Emily like growing dismay. It reminded Emily of how she'd felt—and probably looked—when she'd started in HR, with Steph explaining a filing system that had been alarming in its complexity.

'Don't worry,' she told Helen, squeezing her shoulder. 'You'll get the hang of it in no time. I know it seems overwhelming at first, but it just takes a few calls before it's easy peasy.'

'Easy peasy,' Helen repeated, as if reassuring herself.

'I'll be back in a few hours to check on you,' Emily promised. 'And take you out to lunch.' She wasn't going to make the mistake of skipping lunch again, she thought, even as she acknowledged that

Jason wasn't likely to ask her to dinner two nights in a row.

She hadn't seen him this morning, which was hardly surprising, yet she still felt a tense expectation prickling between her shoulder blades as she took Helen down to reception. It wasn't until she saw Jason come through the front doors of the building that the tension eased and her shoulders relaxed, making Emily realise just what had been causing it in the first place.

'Ah, you must be Helen,' he said, smiling easily as he held a hand out to shake, and Helen's blush deepened so she looked truly lovely, all cream and roses.

'It's so nice to meet you, Mr Kingsley.'

'The pleasure is all mine,' Jason assured her, and his voice had that low, steady thrum that reminded Emily of how he'd been with her last night, how it had made her feel, and she stepped forward, smiling brightly.

'I've just been showing Helen the ropes. But I'm sure she'll be running rings around Jane within hours!' Emily smiled conspiratorially at Jane to let her know this wouldn't *quite* be the case, and Jason turned from Helen to Emily, his gaze resting on her with that quiet sense of assurance that still, after all these years, had the power to unnerve her.

'I'm sure she will, if you have anything to do with it,' he said, and Emily wondered if she was the only one who heard the faintest thread of mocking laughter in his voice. He turned back to Helen, smiling again as he wished her well, and then went to head towards his executive office. After saying her own goodbyes to both receptionists, Emily fell into step with Jason, matching his long stride, and he slid her a sideways glance. 'You seem to be taking quite an interest in Miss Smith.'

'I take an interest in all the people I hire,' Emily replied briskly. 'It's my job.'

'Of course,' Jason agreed. 'And an admirable dedication to your job is the only reason, I suppose?'

He was laughing at her, she knew, but somehow she didn't really mind. She'd reached the door of her office, and she turned to face him, surprised and a bit breathless by how close he stood to her. She could smell the citrusy scent of his aftershave again, and underlying it was a fainter, muskier scent that she knew had to be just *Jason* and the thought made her stomach flip over in a way she was starting to get used to, it had been happening so often in the few days since Jason had returned. Despite its now familiarity, it still felt strange, unnerving, because this was Jason and save the thirty humiliating seconds when she'd asked him to kiss her, she'd never reacted this way to him before. She could only imagine how horrified he would be if he knew. 'Of course,' she said innocently. 'What else would it be?'

'As long as you aren't planning to meddle,' he said. Although he kept his tone light, Emily heard the warning in his words.

'Meddle or matchmake?'

'They're one and the same.'

'Only in your opinion.' She placed a hand on his chest, her palm flattening against the crisp fabric of his shirt, her fingers instinctively seeking the heat of him underneath the cloth. She felt his heart thudding steadily under her palm. She'd meant it to be a light, even impersonal touch, no more than a playful poke in the sternum, yet as if driven by a deeper, baser need, she found it couldn't be that; her hand acted of its own accord, fingers stretching, seeking, while every thought flew from her head.

'You don't need to worry about Helen—or me,' she finally said, fishing for the words that seemed to have pooled deep in her consciousness. She looked up to meet his gaze, saw the gold flecks in his eyes. They weren't brown at all. They weren't boring either. She swallowed. 'You don't need to keep an eye on me, Jason. I'm all grown up now.'

'As I'm coming to realise,' Jason said, his voice so low Emily felt it vibrate through her. His chest tensed under her hand. They remained silent, unmoving, and Emily felt as if everything had slowed down, distilled into this one moment, which was crazy because it wasn't a moment at all. They were just talking. And she was touching his chest.

'Well.' She cleared her throat and somehow managed to remove her hand from his chest; it flopped to her side like a dead thing, useless, awkward, and she suddenly didn't know what to do with it. She was acting ridiculously, Emily thought. Almost as bad as when she'd asked him—

Her mind skittered away from that memory. *Seven years ago*. Old hat, ancient history. Yet it felt close now—far too close—so even now she was half-inclined to tilt her head up and— 'I should get to work,' she said, a little too loudly, and she made her mouth curve into something close to a smile as she turned from him and opened her office door.

Jason watched her go, not moving. It wasn't until she was at her desk that Emily heard him walk down the hall, his steps quick and assured as always, as if he hadn't a care in the world.

She collapsed into her chair. What was *wrong* with her? Why was she acting so strangely around Jason—Jason, who had always been so predictable, so safe, so *ordinary*?

Even as she asked herself the question, Emily knew the answer. She was acting so oddly around Jason—feeling so odd—because no matter how she tried to convince herself otherwise, some vestige of girlish longing from that dance long ago remained inside of her, needing only to see Jason properly again to unfurl and blossom once more.

Some part of her still wanted Jason. Wanted him to kiss her, even. Wanted him the way a woman wanted a man, if only to prove to the girl she'd once been that she was desirable. Desired…by Jason.

Which was ridiculous, because the last person she should be thinking of that way was Jason Kingsley.

He'd surely be appalled if he knew the nature of her thoughts. *She* was appalled, because of all people to be even the littlest bit attracted to—well, Jason Kingsley was low down on her list. Sometimes she wondered if he even liked her all, beyond the most basic affection. He'd certainly always been quick to point out her faults. And as for his faults...well, boring was the least of them. Stodgy and stern and *horribly* practical...

She had no business feeling oddly about him at all. So she wouldn't. It was, Emily decided, a simple matter of mind over body. Whatever latent, leftover feeling she might have secretly nurtured for Jason would be stamped out by self-control right now.

She had more important things to do, better things to think about—

'Emily?'

Emily jerked her head up from where she'd been blindly gazing at a mindless doodle on a spare bit of stationery. It looked suspiciously like a J. She crossed it out viciously and then smiled at the woman who stood in her doorway, her skirt six inches shorter than Emily's, her nails curved talons, ruthlessly manicured. Gillian Bateson, the Head of Public Relations.

'Gillian, hello. Good to see you. Can I help with something?'

'I don't suppose Stephanie told you about the charity fund-raiser?' Gillian said in that rather lofty tone that Emily had never liked.

'I'm afraid not,' she replied equably enough. She knew the basics: every year Jason hosted an exclusive fund-raiser for a water-based charity, usually in one of London's best hotels. It was an intimate, expensive event that Gillian organised, apparently with help from HR.

'It's a very big do,' Gillian said, seating herself down across from Emily. 'Last year we raised three million pounds for wells in the Sudan.'

'That must have made for a lot of wells,' Emily said politely. She just managed to keep the mischief from her voice. Gillian had always been rather full of her own importance.

'It's a *very* important event,' Gillian confirmed, rolling her eyes dramatically. 'Of course, I'm in charge of it since it's essentially PR, but Stephanie always wanted to know what was going on—I suppose I'll have to fill you in, as well?' She made it sound as if that would be a terribly tiresome thing to do, and Emily smiled in understanding.

'If you'd be so kind, Gillian.' She had to remind herself that Gillian had been divorced three times and had lost custody of her only daughter. All the nail varnish and hairspray surely hid a deep heartache. Or so she tried to believe.

'Well…' Yet another eye roll. If she kept at it, Emily thought wryly, she'd have her eyes permanently aimed at the back of her head. 'We're raising money for a desalination plant in Namibia. The fund-raiser is meant to have a black and white theme, and since Jason's flat is decorated in black and white we're going to have it there—'

'The fund-raiser is at Jason's flat?' Emily could not keep the surprise from her voice as she digested this information, unsure how she felt about it. Or Gillian calling him by his first name in that intimate way.

Gillian arched her ruthlessly plucked eyebrows, a smug smile curving that over-lipsticked mouth. 'You *have* been there?'

Actually, she hadn't. And no doubt Gillian knew it. She'd been there, obviously. Emily did not want to ask herself why. She smiled, shaking her head regretfully. 'No, I'm afraid I haven't had the honour, but I'm sure it's stunning. And Mr Kingsley is certainly generous to lend the use of his flat for the fund-raiser.'

'Yes, he is, isn't he?' Gillian swung one foot, her spiked heel dangling. 'I don't know why he hasn't married,' she mused.

'I'm sure he hasn't found someone sensible enough for him,' Emily said, her voice sharpening for the first time, and Gillian gave her a knowing glance.

'You think he needs someone sensible? He's hardly gone for the sensible types before.'

Emily shifted in her seat, uncomfortable with the nature of the conversation, or the sharp stab of something that felt almost like jealousy at the thought of Jason *going* for anyone.

Still, Emily was forced to acknowledge that

Gillian was right. Jason had never taken out sensible types, but then he'd never been seen with the same woman twice. All they'd been were dates, just as he'd said. Arm candy. So just what kind of woman would he want to be the mother of his all-important heir? What woman would fall in line with his no-love qualification? Plenty of women, Emily supposed, including sweetly biddable Helen Smith or worldly Gillian Bateson.

And why, oh, why, was she thinking like this?

'In any case,' Gillian said with another cat-like smile, 'I'm sure he's getting ready to settle down. He's quite a catch.'

'I suppose.' What awful expressions, Emily thought. A catch, like you had to run after somebody and wrestle them to the ground before convincing him to marry you. And settling down was even worse. It sounded so…disappointing. She could just imagine what kind of woman Jason would choose: someone coolly composed and perhaps just a little bit horsey; someone who would arrange flowers and place settings with contemptuous ease and give him an heir and a spare right off the bat. She'd have no sense of humour at all. A woman like that would be perfect for Jason. She would be so very sensible and stodgy, just as he was.

Except he hadn't seemed so stodgy last night.

'Well, that's probably all you need to know,' Gillian said, unfolding herself from the chair. 'The head of every department gets an invite, but that's all.' So that was why she'd never been to one of Jason's fund-raisers before, Emily thought a bit sourly. Gillian strode towards the door. 'I'll take care of all the arrangements. You can just show up.' Emily had a feeling Gillian was keeping her out of the loop on purpose, especially since the fund-raiser would be at Jason's flat. No doubt Gillian had her eye on him as husband number four.

And that unpleasant feeling still spiking through her was *not* jealousy. Emily gave Gillian her sunniest smile. 'Thank you so much, Gillian, that's lovely.' She breathed a sigh of relief when Gillian finally stalked out of the room, leaving behind a waft of cloying perfume.

Emily let out a tiny sigh. Why was she irritated by Jason's offer to host the party? Or was it simply the possessive way Gillian had talked about Jason—as well as the thought of him finding a wife?

None of it had anything to do with her, and it shouldn't affect her mood at all. It wouldn't, because she wouldn't let it. Determinedly, Emily turned back to her desk and she spent the rest of the morning taking telephone calls and sending emails, purposefully busy, before she headed down to the reception area to meet Helen for lunch as promised.

'How are things going?' she asked cheerfully as she approached the circular marble desk that was the focal point of the building's lobby. Jane was busy on a call, but Helen sat there looking pale and a bit woebegone. 'Got the hang of it?' Emily asked, smiling, and Helen darted an anxious look at Jane.

'I disconnected three calls,' she confessed in a whisper. 'And I got the lists wrong—'

'The lists?'

'The ones about who likes their calls and who doesn't,' Helen explained. She sounded frantic. 'I mixed it all up, and gave the calls to people who don't want them and not to those who do—'

'Oh, well, no one was too bothered, were they?' Emily said, quick to reassure Helen. 'I told you, we're quite a friendly bunch here.'

'Mr Hatley came down right to the desk,' Helen said in a low voice. 'Shouted at me that he didn't want the bloody calls.' She blinked up at Emily, who felt her heart give a little twist at Helen's obvious misery.

'I should have warned you about John,' she said. 'He's an old bear, but his bark is much worse than his bite. Or growl, I suppose. Come on.' She reached for Helen's coat, which hung on a nearby hook, and handed it to her. 'There's a pasta place around the corner that does a wonderful lasagne. Let's forget our troubles for a bit.'

Helen rose gratefully from her seat and Emily waved to Jane, who gave her a rather despairing shake of her head and a pointed look at Helen before Emily sailed through the building's front doors. It appeared it was going to take more than a morning for Helen to figure out the phones, but she'd get there in the end. Emily would make sure of it.

In any case, everything looked better from a cosy table in a restaurant, as they tucked into huge bowls of pasta and crusty garlic bread.

'How are you finding London?' Emily asked as she twirled some linguine around her fork. 'Is Richard showing you around a bit?'

'A bit,' Helen allowed. She sounded cautious, perhaps even unhappy. Emily could hardly pretend to be surprised.

'He's busy, I suppose?' she said in sympathy; she could just imagine Richard getting on with his flood retention basins and hydraulic mechanisms and who knew what else, leaving Helen quite on her own.

'I didn't realise he worked quite as much as he did,' Helen admitted. 'And I don't understand a word of it—'

'Neither do I,' Emily confessed cheerfully. 'And I've worked here for five years.' She was interested in people, not mathematical formulas or desalination plants, for that matter. 'Surely he's been around sometimes, though?' she asked, and Helen gave a little shrug.

'Occasionally,' she said softly. She hesitated, then confessed in an anxious rush, 'I suppose it's bound to be different than you think, isn't it? We've been friends for so long, you know, and of course things will be bumpy at first—'

Bumpy? Emily felt a swell of self-righteous

indignation. Surely Helen deserved a bit better than *bumpy*, a little more than sitting at home waiting for Richard to ring. 'Tell you what,' she said suddenly, an idea lighting her mind and firing her heart, 'I've an invitation to a party tonight—it's a launch for a new clothing designer, I think.' Actually, she wasn't sure what it was for; she received dozens of invitations every week, so that Emily mixed them up in her mind. Yet any of them would be a good opportunity to dance and laugh, and that was just what Helen needed. 'Why don't you come with me?'

Helen's face slackened in shock. 'Me? You want to go with *me*?'

Richard had already done a number on her, Emily thought sourly. 'Of course. It'll be fun.'

'I don't have proper clothes—'

'You can borrow something of mine.' Emily eyed Helen assessingly, acknowledging that she was probably a size or two smaller than Emily was. Well, she had a few things she didn't fit into any more, alas. And the idea of a makeover energised her. 'We'll have a real girly evening getting all done up,' she said, 'and then have a night on the town! Richard won't know what's happened to you.'

Slowly, shyly, Helen brightened. 'That does sound lovely,' she began, 'but—'

'No buts. It will be fun.' And successful, as Jason liked to say. Quickly, she pushed him out of her mind. He didn't need to know about this.

By eight o'clock that night Emily was shepherding

Helen into the foyer of one of London's grandest hotels. Helen was looking around in awe, clearly overwhelmed by the sheer luxury of the venue, with its glittering chandeliers and marble floor, the ballroom bustling with a thousand guests, all of them well-connected and wealthy.

Helen had transformed into a swan quite wonderfully, Emily thought in satisfaction. The black cocktail dress was unfortunately two years out of date as it was one of the only things of hers that had fitted Helen, but its lines were simple and classic and made the most of the younger woman's slight frame. Emily had piled her luxuriant dark hair on top of her head, and emphasised Helen's huge grey eyes with dark shadow and eyeliner. And she'd given her a manicure. She looked gorgeous.

Buoyed by her own efforts, Emily worked her way through the crowd, plucking two flutes of champagne from a circulating tray as she introduced Helen to the numerous acquaintances she'd cultivated over the years. No matter that Helen mumbled her greetings as she ducked her head; she'd get the hang of it soon, and she was pretty enough that it hardly mattered what she said.

'How have I missed you two gorgeous ladies?' A smooth voice interrupted Emily's latest introduction and she turned to see Philip Ellsworth standing just a little too close, his gaze taking in Helen even as he smiled at Emily. Philip was charming, wealthy and definitely had an eye for the ladies. Emily watched

Helen blush under Philip's appreciative stare. Well, her confidence could use a little bolstering.

'*So* charmed to meet you,' Philip said after Emily had made the necessary introductions. 'I can't believe I haven't come across you before. I'm sure I would have remembered.'

'Helen is new to London,' Emily interjected. Philip was still gazing at Helen with obvious admiration, and it compelled her to say, 'The music is just starting up. Philip, I'm sure Helen would love to dance.' All right, it was a little obvious, but he clearly enjoyed her company, and why shouldn't Helen have a dance? 'You do like to dance, don't you, Helen?'

'Yes,' Helen admitted in a shy whisper.

'In that case, I'll have to oblige,' Philip said with a charming and very white smile. He must use artificial whitener, Emily thought with a tiny flicker of distaste. Yet there could be no denying he was incredibly handsome and suave. And just the thing to cheer Helen up a bit. 'I'm always at Emily's command,' he added, throwing Emily a sleek and even sly look. She firmly ignored it.

'Go on, then,' she said, and watched in satisfaction as Philip led Helen to the dance floor with obvious expertise. And Helen wasn't too bad a dancer herself. Who knew what could happen there, Emily mused. Philip was in his thirties. Perhaps he was looking to marry, as well. Settle down. She smiled wryly at her own choice of words. No doubt Jason would accuse her of matchmaking again, but she could hardly be blamed if Helen and Philip made a go of it—

Emily laughed aloud. Those unfortunate phrases really had got stuck in her head. Her gaze returned to Philip and Helen. He was holding her quite close, and she was looking up at him with a rather dazed smile. Emily could not suppress the sharp stab of triumph at seeing Helen out and enjoying herself, flourishing under the approval and attraction of a handsome man. Take that, Richard Marsden.

She lifted her champagne flute, only to pause with it halfway to her lips as her body tensed of its own accord, a shiver of awareness rippling over her. She felt as if she were being watched, and before her brain had processed this her body already knew.

Her gaze swivelled to the entrance of the ballroom and she felt as if an electric current had just pinned her in place. Jason Kingsley stood there, and he was looking right at her.

CHAPTER FIVE

EMILY took a hasty sip of her champagne, then promptly choked, causing an ageing socialite to give her a frosty frown. Such behaviour was hardly decorous.

Emily smiled weakly and watched as Jason made his way towards her, threading through the well-heeled crowd with an arrogant assurance, seemingly indifferent to the people mingling around him. He was a head taller than most of them, and they looked no more than a swarm of insects buzzing about him, an annoyance he dealt with easily as he made his way towards her. Emily swallowed, her chest still burning from when she'd choked. Jason didn't look angry precisely, but he didn't look happy either. Nervously, her gaze flicked to Helen and Philip, now swaying to the music. She had a feeling he wouldn't be happy about that.

Jason surveyed Emily and tried not to scowl. She wore a tiny slip of a silver spangled dress that glittered like water on the scales of a fish, her hair falling down her back in golden waves. She looked, he thought, like an X-rated mermaid.

'What a surprise to see you here,' she said, tilting her head and giving him a flirty smile, her cat's eyes slanted at the corners, alight with mischief.

Jason held on to his temper, but just. He'd arrived a few minutes ago with Margaret Denton, a girl he'd gone to Cambridge with and who was now a solicitor, very elegant, understated and perfect wife material. And then he'd seen Emily…and Helen. He'd watched as Emily pushed Helen towards Philip Ellsworth, who was the biggest waste of space Jason had ever encountered and was steadily partying his way through his daddy's trust fund. Jason's annoyance had increased as Philip took Helen to the dance floor and Emily practically preened with satisfaction. She was matchmaking. Again. And this time she—or at least Helen—was quite out of her element. He'd left Margaret with a cluster of mutual acquaintances and headed towards Emily, drawn to her with a force he could neither stem nor stop.

He smiled at her now, coolly. 'I do attend social events, Emily,' he said, keeping his voice mild, 'although perhaps not as many as you do.' He nodded towards Helen and Ellsworth. 'Now I *am* surprised to see her here.'

'I invited her,' Emily informed him with a hint of defiance beneath her blithe tone. 'I thought she could use a night out—'

'Don't you think this might be a bit much?' Jason

surveyed the crowd with a jaundiced eye. Most of the guests were shallow, petty, vain and insipid. And they'd devour Helen Smith in one bite.

'It's just a good time,' Emily said with a defensive shrug. 'And it's better than Helen waiting for Richard Marsden to ring.'

'You've really got it in for him, haven't you?' Jason said. He took a flute of champagne from a tray and downed half of it in one sip. He'd never seen a dress quite as revealing as Emily's. Her legs looked endless, ending in silver skyscraper heels. She'd painted her toenails silver to match. He yanked his gaze upwards, but there was no hope to be found there. Admittedly, the dress wasn't particularly low cut, but the silver material moulded itself to Emily's breasts, outlining every luscious curve. He settled his scowl on Emily's face, for he was indeed scowling now. She seemed to have that effect on him.

'I don't have it in for anyone,' Emily told him, sounding defensive. 'But I don't see any harm in inviting Helen out—'

'And are you going to pretend you didn't just push her towards Ellsworth?'

Emily flushed, and Jason couldn't help but notice how the heightened colour brightened her eyes. Her chest heaved, drawing his attention downwards again. His scowl deepened. 'All I did was ask him to dance with her—'

'Usually, it's the man who does the asking.'

'This is the twenty-first century, in case that had escaped your notice—'

'You're matchmaking again, Emily,' Jason cut her off softly. 'And this time I'd really rather you wouldn't.'

'Why? You're matchmaking as much as I am, clearing the way so she can be with someone like Richard.'

Jason stilled, every muscle tensed. He didn't like her scoffing tone. Or her implication. 'Someone like Richard?' he repeated, his voice lowering dangerously. He *felt* dangerous.

'Yes,' Emily replied with some heat, 'someone earnest and dull who can't be bothered to romance the woman he allegedly loves—'

'You've witnessed this? Talked to Richard, perhaps?'

Emily's flush deepened. 'It's fairly obvious from talking to Helen,' she finally said. She bit her lip, taking its fullness between her teeth, and Jason's fingers clenched around his flute of champagne.

'What does it matter to you?' he demanded roughly. 'I didn't think you were a great believer in love anyway.'

'I do believe in love!' Emily returned with sudden force. Her voice rose and Jason wished he had thought to have this conversation somewhere more private. She was making a scene. 'I believe in it very much,' she continued, her voice thankfully a notch lower. 'Just because I haven't found it for myself—'

'But you're looking after all?' Jason enquired. Why was he asking? Why did he *care?*

Emily looked troubled, and trapped. She lifted one shoulder in a shrug, and the skinny strap of her dress fell down her arm. Her dress had just become a bit more revealing. 'I'm happy as I am,' she said firmly, 'and I don't have anything against Richard Marsden.'

Jason's mouth curved in a cool smile. 'No, indeed, you just find him—let me think—*boring.* Predictable. Cautious.'

Emily stiffened in surprise, her eyes widening. 'This isn't about you, Jason.'

No, it wasn't, Jason thought savagely. Yet it *felt* like it was about him, and her rather dire assessment of him that still, stupidly, stung. Deliberately, he reached out and slid the strap back up to her shoulder, his fingers sliding along her skin. Emily jerked in response, and he saw desire flare in her eyes. A feeling of triumph raced through him, headier than champagne, followed by another flash of lust. He smiled. 'No, of course not,' he murmured. 'It's not about you or me at all.' His hand lingered on her shoulder, his thumb tracing the arc of her collarbone. Emily had frozen, staring at him in dazed shock, and Jason knew he should remove his hand. He was doing it again. Playing with fire. Yet he just couldn't seem to stop.

* * *

Emily felt as if her mind and body had both frozen, so shocked by the way Jason was touching her. Although that wasn't quite true; all he'd done was fix her dress strap. No, she was shocked by her own response, the desire coursing through her in a molten flood she had neither expected nor experienced before. And she couldn't move—or think—or even breathe. The crowds shifted and swirled around them, and she felt as if she and Jason were pinned in place. His thumb stroked her collarbone again, his eyes hard and blazing on hers.

Somehow, slowly, as if she were in quicksand, Emily moved. She took a shaky step backwards, shaking her head with more force than intended or necessary, her champagne sloshing and her hair flying. 'This argument is pointless,' she said. 'Helen is a grown woman and she can do as she likes. And so can Richard—and Philip—and you.' Jason had dropped his hand and was simply staring at her. Too disconcerted to say anything more, Emily gave him one last pointed look and pivoted on her heel, intent on finding the only safety on offer: the Ladies.

Yet just as she'd entered the empty, quiet corridor that led to the loos, Jason was there, his long strides overtaking Emily's, so he cut her off from her escape and with the simple turn of his body left her trapped against a wall.

'Jason—'

His body was close enough that she could feel the heat of him, sense his strength. 'You're absolutely right, Emily, Helen can do as she likes. And so can Ellsworth. And Richard. And me.' She looked up at him, his face alarmingly close to hers. His hair was rumpled and colour slashed his cheekbones. Emily was conscious of his nearness, the very scent of him, the way his chest rose and fell under the crisp whiteness of his shirt. Her mind spun with the sensory overload, blanking as she stared up at him, felt the heat of his body like a pulse against her own.

He braced his hands against the wall on either side of her head so that she was effectively imprisoned, although standing between the strength of his arms did not feel like being trapped. Instead, as her heart started to pound and her cheeks flushed, Emily felt a glorious sense of anticipation that rose up inside her like a bubble, so she felt almost as if she could float right off the ground, anchored only by the heavy thud of her heart. Jason's gaze remained on her, his eyes the colour of dark honey, and Emily could not look away. From somewhere she found words.

'Well, of course, Jason, they can all do as they like.' She looked up at him, felt her lips part in what surely was expectation. *Invitation*. Her voice lowered to a breathless, husky murmur. 'And just what is it you'd like to do?'

'This.'

As he lowered his head to hers, Emily could hardly believe this was happening. He was going to kiss her. Alarmingly. Amazingly. At last.

And then he *was* kissing her, his lips cool and

firm on hers, one hand coming to curve possessively about her waist, his fingers splaying along her hip. With his other hand he touched her cheek, cradling her face in a gesture that was as intimate as the kiss itself and infinitely more tender.

Emily remained frozen under that gentle touch of his lips, too shocked to respond, at least at first. Then her body began to become aware of just how wonderful it felt to be kissed by Jason, every nerve and sinew suddenly, gloriously alive, overwhelmed by a tidal wave of sensation. As Jason gently explored the contours of her lips, his mouth so firm and persuasive on hers, her body clamoured for more and then took control despite the sputtering protests her mind still insisted on making.

This is Jason—Jason! He can't be kissing me. He can't want to kiss me...

Her body was defiant; Emily found she was taking hold of Jason's shoulders, almost as if she meant to push him away, except of course she didn't. Instead, her hands slid from his shoulders to his head, her fingers threading through the crisp softness of his hair as her mouth opened under his like a flower in the sun and the gentle touch of his tongue to hers sent her body spinning into a deeper whirlpool of sudden, intense feeling.

Yet Jason did not deepen the kiss further and, even as she pressed closer, her hips bumping his, she became aware of his restraint. He did not pull her closer; he did not move at all and as her brain came up to speed with her body, Emily realised this kiss was not a kiss of passion, but one of proof. Jason was proving something to her; he was telling her something with this kiss, and Emily wasn't sure it was anything she wanted to hear.

Yet before she could pull away in appalled indignation, which was what she intended, Jason broke the kiss and stepped away with his own cool little smile. Emily stared at him, her chest heaving, her lips tingling.

'What was that for?' she demanded in a raw voice.

He looked nonplussed for a tiny beat before his lips curved wider in a satisfied smile. 'Does there need to be a purpose?'

Emily had no answer, because now that her body had stopped its restless clamour—although it still *ached*—her mind had taken over, spinning out incoherent protests, impossible ideas.

'Very well,' Jason said coolly, his voice edged with impatience. 'Then this. Now you know I'm not boring… and neither is Richard Marsden.'

'And a kiss is meant to convince me of that?' Emily scoffed, which would have been a lot more believable if her voice hadn't wobbled.

'Considering how much you enjoyed it,' Jason replied, his gaze sweeping over her flushed face and heaving chest with knowing assessment, 'yes.'

'I didn't—' Emily protested uselessly, for it was surely a lie and Jason was already walking away from her.

Jason stalked away from Emily, furious with himself for losing his self-control. For kissing her. And yet his body wanted—demanded—more, and he was both aggravated and amazed by how that one simple kiss had affected him so much. Affected her as well, to both his satisfaction and shame.

'Jason, where *have* you been?' Eyebrows arched, too elegant to look annoyed, Margaret Denton glided up to him, one thin hand on his arm, her nails biting into his flesh. The smile she gave him was both imperious and reproving, and annoyed him all the more. She smiled as if she were his mother, as if she already owned him.

And this was a woman he was considering for his *wife*?

Not any more.

Carefully, Jason detached his arm from Margaret's biting grasp. 'I'm sorry, Margaret, I had business to attend to.' She pursed her lips, unimpressed, and Jason's gaze settled on the woman across the ballroom who stood alone, watching the crowds with a lonely longing. 'Excuse me,' he told Margaret and, without looking back, he headed across the ballroom.

'Mr Kingsley!' Helen Smith looked at him in both surprise and more than a little relief. How long had she been standing alone? Jason wondered. How long had it taken Ellsworth to ditch her?

'Good evening, Helen. I hope you're having a good time?'

'Oh…yes.' She smiled, but he saw the uncertainty in her eyes. This kind of crowd was far from her own experience, and standing alone like a wallflower had to be a miserable introduction to it.

'I wonder if you could do me a favour,' Jason said, and Helen nodded, her eyes wide.

'Of…of course—'

'Emily wasn't feeling all that well, and I believe she's gone to the Ladies. Would you mind checking on her?' He glanced at his watch as if he cared what time it was. 'I'm afraid I have to run.'

'Of course, Mr Kingsley—'

Smiling his thanks, Jason turned to leave the ballroom behind. He'd done enough damage for one night.

Emily stood in the elegantly upholstered ladies' room, gazing at her shocked reflection in the gilt mirror. Her face was flushed, her lips reddened, her hair a tousled mess. She looked as if that one kiss—just one kiss!—had utterly affected her, changed her, and in some ways it had.

Jason Kingsley had kissed her. Why? What had he been hoping to accomplish? He'd certainly never expressed any interest in kissing her before—and after he'd kissed her he'd stepped away so easily, giving her such a cool little smile.

Emily felt her stomach lurch in panicked protest. He wasn't interested in kissing her at all. He hadn't been affected like she was, even now, her face flushed and her mind spinning in dazed, dizzying circles.

The door to the ladies' room opened and Helen slipped in, frowning in hesitant concern. 'Emily—are you all right?'

Emily pushed her hair behind her ears and lifted her chin. 'Of course. Why shouldn't I be?'

'It's just that Mr Kingsley said you were in the Ladies and I ought to check on you—'

'Jason worries too much,' Emily said with a laugh that sounded just a bit brittle. It both stung and soothed her that Jason had thought it necessary to send someone to check on her. It was considerate—and annoying. He'd probably been trying to detach Helen from Philip, and this was simply an excuse. 'Honestly, I'm fine. The noise is giving me a bit of a headache, that's all.' She ran some water over her wrists and then quite deliberately took her lipstick from her handbag and reapplied it, her gaze fixed firmly on her own reflection. Her blush had faded, she saw, and her lips did not look so swollen. Slipping the lipstick back into her bag, she turned to Helen. 'There. Shall we go back out?' Helen nodded and Emily smiled, her equanimity almost restored as she led the way back to the ballroom. 'Philip

Ellsworth is very nice, isn't he?' she said, and from the corner of her eye she saw Helen blush and felt another little stab of satisfaction.

Take that, Jason Kingsley, she thought and, smiling, reached for another glass of champagne. She glanced around the ballroom, instinctively seeking out that tall, purposeful figure but she could tell from the emptiness she felt inside that Jason had already gone.

Emily kept her thoughts from Jason—and that kiss—for the rest of the evening. She was on full form, sparkling and chatting and posing for photographs until well after midnight, when common sense finally told her she—as well as Helen—had to return to work tomorrow, so they might as well call it a night.

Yet, alone in her flat, the rooms all dark around her, she found the memory of Jason's kiss came rushing back to her, overwhelming her senses and making her ache deep inside in a way she didn't like but recognised as the onslaught of unfulfilled desire.

Why had Jason kissed her? Why had it stirred up this longing and need inside of her, when surely it couldn't be sated? *She* couldn't. Not by Jason, for that kiss—that little kiss—had been nothing more than a proof, a punishment for pushing Helen and Philip together.

The more Emily considered it, the more she felt, like a leaden lump in the pit of her stomach, that she was right. Jason had not kissed her out of desire or attraction or anything like that. He'd kissed her to prove something to her, simply because he could. The thought sent a blush firing Emily's body and scorching her face, even in the empty darkness of her own flat. She was reminded, painfully, of Jason's rejection on the dance floor seven years ago. She'd so desperately wanted to prove to him—and herself— how beyond that moment she was, how grown-up and sophisticated and worldly she'd become, but she'd done the opposite. Now, with the aftermath of that kiss sending a riot of ricocheting emotions through her, Emily realised she wasn't sophisticated at all... at least not when it came to Jason. With Jason she would forever be an adoring, annoying little girl, and she'd never felt so more than now.

Jason stared at the social pages of the newspaper that his PA had laid out with other relevant articles. Tumbled, golden curls, a tiny silver scrap of a dress. Three separate photographs, each one more damning than the last. He scanned the captions: *Emily Wood dazzles the fund-raising scene in an exclusively designed dress... Emily Wood and unidentified guest toast their evening... Emily Wood and Philip Ellsworth dance together at last night's charity gala.*

With a grimace of disgust, Jason pushed the pages away. He didn't need to see any more photographs. He'd already been convinced that as charming as

Emily was, as desirable as he knew her to be, she could also be silly, scatty and most unsuitable. He had no business expressing any interest in her at all. No business kissing her.

She was not wife material. Not even close.

So why couldn't he get her out of his mind? Why couldn't he forget that kiss?

Why did he want more?

He'd returned to London for the express purpose of finding a wife. With his father's health failing, it had become all the more urgent. He had no time to waste with Emily Wood, and yet he was honest enough to realise he had trouble resisting her. His self-control had deserted him, his willpower at an all-time low. How he'd managed to keep his distance from Emily for seven years he had no idea, since he certainly couldn't seem to manage it any longer.

With another grimace Jason pressed the intercom for his PA. 'Book my ticket for Nairobi, Eloise,' he said. 'I'm going back to Africa after all.'

By the next morning, Emily had pushed the kiss and all its accompanying realisations completely out of her mind. Almost. He still lingered on the fringes of her consciousness like a mist, and she found herself gazing blankly at her computer while her hand went inadvertently to touch her lips, remembering the touch of his mouth against hers, how firmly his lips had moved over hers, that thrilling touch of his tongue and the very taste of him—

Stop. She had to stop. Yet, despite her determination not to, she spent the entire morning in a state of high tension, waiting to see Jason, preparing herself for the pointed barbs he would no doubt direct her way. Yet he did not stop by her office and despite her half-dozen forays to the lobby—to check on Helen, of course—she did not see him enter the building. At lunch his PA informed her that Jason was out of the office for a few days, preparing for another trip to Africa.

'I thought he was back for a while,' Emily said, hating that she actually sounded disappointed. 'A few months, at least.'

The PA, Eloise, shrugged. 'An emergency came up.'

Emily stopped by Helen's desk on the way back upstairs. 'Richard's going off to Africa again?' she said, and Helen nodded, her expression downcast.

'Yes, it's very important, he said. Just a week, though, this time.'

'Well, that's good, then,' Emily said after a moment. 'Did you have fun last night?'

'Yes—' Helen smiled rather shyly, and Emily smiled back in encouragement, sensing the younger woman wanted to say something more. 'Philip is very nice,' she finally admitted in a whisper, and Emily felt a thrill of triumph—as well as trepidation. Suddenly she was glad Jason wasn't in the office today.

'He is,' she said after a second's pause. 'Perhaps you'll see him again.'

'Do you think?' Helen's face lit up even as she chewed her lip nervously. Emily felt another flicker of trepidation. Philip really was charming, she told herself. Yes, he moved in a fast crowd, but he was always unfailingly polite—if a little smooth—and she'd never heard anything *that* bad about him. Helen, with her sweetness and innocence, could be perfect for him. Surely there was nothing wrong with enabling them to spend a little time together.

With another smile directed at Helen, she headed back up to her office. Work took up too much of her time to think about Jason, or anyone else for that matter. When the phone rang at the end of the day, she was surprised to hear Philip's plummy tone.

'Philip! You've never rung me at work before.'

'There's a first time for everything.'

Emily leaned back in her chair, anticipation racing through her. Philip had never rung her before at all, and there could only be one reason—one person— why he would do so now. 'So what's the occasion?' she asked.

'No occasion. I have spare theatre tickets and, after seeing you and your lovely companion last night, I thought you might want to go with me.'

'The theatre? I'm sure that would be lovely.' Of course he didn't know Helen well enough to ask her alone, Emily thought, her excitement mounting. She was the perfect cover. He really was interested in

Helen. After making arrangements with Philip, she disconnected the call and hurried downstairs to tell Helen the news.

Several hours later they were having drinks in the theatre bar, waiting for the curtain. Philip was charming as always, and had even kissed Helen's cheek when he'd seen her. Emily stepped away so she was on the other side of the little table, and Philip and Helen sat next to each other on tall stools. Philip, Emily decided firmly, would be just the right man for Helen. He'd wine her and dine her and sweep her off her feet, just as she deserved. And Emily could show Jason how wrong he was. Now *that* thought was immensely satisfying. All it would take was a little nudge in the right direction...

For a moment Emily felt a ripple of concern for the hapless and absent Richard. She really didn't have anything against him, did she? No, of course not. If Richard wanted to be with Helen, he could certainly make a bit more effort. Perhaps Philip's attention towards Helen would motivate him. Or... She glanced at the pair across from her; Philip was tucking a tendril of hair behind Helen's ear while she ducked her head and blushed. Or Philip and Helen could fall in love and live happily ever after, the way it was supposed to happen. The way her parents had, until her mother had died.

The way she wanted for herself, even if she'd told

Jason otherwise. Even if she was afraid that she'd never find that kind of man, that kind of love.

The bell rang, and Emily stood up from the table. The show was about to begin.

Emily's mood remained buoyant throughout the evening and all the way home. Philip had suggested they all share a cab, but Emily had insisted she could walk and left the two of them speeding away in the darkness. She imagined telling Jason the news that Philip and Helen were together, even engaged. She pictured the huge wedding, hundreds of guests. Perhaps she'd even be bridesmaid. She'd wear something understated, and look modest and quietly proud—

Chuckling softly at her own flight of fancy, Emily let herself into her flat. Her mobile phone buzzed with a message and Emily flipped it open as she shed her coat and kicked off her heels. There were two messages which she'd missed while at the theatre: one from her sister, asking her if she was coming to Surrey for Christmas, and then another from Stephanie, reminding her of the rehearsal dinner for her wedding in two weeks' time. Emily could hardly believe the wedding was so soon. She wondered if Jason would be attending, and then quickly banished that thought. It hardly mattered anyway.

Emily was dying to know how the evening turned out for Philip and Helen, and she finally got the low-down when she stopped by reception on the way to lunch the next day. Helen was getting ready to leave for an afternoon appointment at the dentist's and they walked out together into the brisk November afternoon.

'So…' was all Emily needed to say for Helen to launch into a hesitant yet happy description of Philip and all his charms.

'He's so gorgeous, isn't he?' Helen said with a sigh. 'And he says the funniest things…and he looks at me as if he likes me…' She paused, nibbling her lip, her lashes sweeping downward for a moment before she looked up anxiously at Emily. 'He looks at me and I go all tingly. I feel so *alive*. Have you ever felt like that?'

'Alive?' Emily repeated dryly. 'Yes, I think so.'

'I meant—'

'I know,' Emily said quickly, suppressing a pang of remorse at her rather facetious reply. 'And to tell you the truth, Helen, I've never felt like that with a man.' She thought briefly of Jason's kiss, and hurriedly suppressed the memory. Her two dismal attempts at a relationship hardly counted either. No, love looked set to pass her by, and that was fine. Hearing about it from Helen was good enough. Almost, anyway. She smiled down at her. 'So what you've got must be special.'

'Do you think so?' Helen asked. 'Do you think he likes me?'

Emily thought of the way Philip had sat next to Helen, had brushed her hair away from her face, had slid next to her in the cab, their thighs touching. 'I'm sure of it,' she said.

'Richard will be so disappointed,' Helen said quietly. 'We were meant to use this time to get to know one another—to see if we suit—'

'And obviously you don't,' Emily replied briskly. 'If he'd wanted to be with you so much, he should have asked you out. Sent you flowers—'

'He did give me a house plant,' Helen said quickly, and Emily only just kept herself from rolling her eyes.

'How very nice of him,' she said. 'Still, it's not your fault if you don't…suit. And since Philip is here and Richard isn't…'

'He leaves for Africa tomorrow,' Helen said in a low voice. 'I should tell him, I know, but…' She nibbled her lip again and Emily smiled kindly.

'But?'

'We've been friends for so long,' Helen said. She sounded miserable. 'And Richard really is a nice man—'

'Of course he is. But you don't date—or marry—someone just because he's nice. I think you need a bit more than that, Helen. You deserve it.'

'Do I?'

'Yes,' she told her firmly, 'you do.' Every woman did. Helen was just one of the lucky ones who might actually get it.

Helen nodded, accepting, and Emily waved her off to her dentist's appointment, expansively offering to let her take the rest of the afternoon off. 'I know what that novocaine can do to you. You'd be lisping into the phone!'

'I should be back by four,' Helen said. 'I don't want to leave Jane in the lurch. And actually I kind of enjoy the work now.' Smiling with a new self-confidence, Helen headed down the street. Emily watched her, feeling proud of Helen and all she'd accomplished, and yet…she could not keep a strange, empty feeling from rattling around inside her. She felt a little forlorn, a little lonely, as she headed up to her office. She knew she should be happy for Helen, and she was, of course she was. Yet as she sank into her chair she also realised she felt a bit adrift herself. She had since Jason had kissed her and scattered all her certainties. *I'm happy as I am.*

Was she? Was she really?

Staring blankly at her computer screen, Emily wasn't sure she was any more. The thought was frightening. Depressing too. Because if she wasn't happy, what on earth could she do about it?

Forcing the question—and its impossible answer—aside, she kept her head down and focused on work until a hesitant knock on her door at half past three. She looked up and stared straight at Richard Marsden.

'Hello,' he began, awkward and uncertain, and Emily simply stared, shock rendering her temporarily speechless. A creeping sense of discomfort immediately followed, for while she'd been telling

Helen it was perfectly fine to forget Richard just hours ago, she hadn't had to deal with the man face to face.

Now he stood here in an ill-fitting suit, round-shouldered and a little dull, yet, Emily acknowledged fairly, with a rather nice smile.

'Sorry to bother you, but I'm looking for Helen Smith. Jane down at reception said you might know where she is.'

'She's at the dentist's,' Emily said, her voice faintly cool despite her intention to sound both friendly and professional.

'Oh.' Richard's face fell, the corners of his mouth turning down almost comically. 'I was hoping to catch her before I leave for Africa. I'd stop by her flat but my flight leaves at eight—' He paused hopefully and Emily did not attempt to fill the silence. 'Do you know if she'll be back today?'

Emily hesitated. Clearly Helen had not told Jane that she intended to return by four. Of course, Helen's appointment could run long—dentist appointments often did—and there was no saying for certain that she would be back in the office today. There was no saying for certain at all.

Emily looked at Richard Marsden's slightly droopy eyes, his kind smile, and then quite suddenly pictured Jason saying coolly, *You most certainly are not in the running.* She remembered how easily he'd walked away from that kiss, and how shattered she'd felt in its aftermath.

Her own mouth hardened and she heard herself saying, 'I'm afraid I don't know, Richard. She told me she planned to take the entire afternoon off.'

Richard nodded slowly in acceptance, clearly defeated before he'd even begun. Emily felt a flicker of regret but also a stab of self-righteous scorn. If Richard wasn't going to try harder than *that*—

'Well, if you see her, will you tell her I stopped by? And that…that I'm thinking of her?'

Emily knew she would have no difficulty in delivering Richard's paltry message. 'Of course I will.'

'Thank you,' he said, and Emily, her throat suddenly tight, just nodded.

As he rounded the corner, she managed to call out, 'Have a safe trip, Richard.'

Then, as he finally disappeared down the hallway, she let out a long, slow breath she hadn't realised she'd been holding.

It didn't matter, she told herself. Helen would have said something to Richard anyway. She was planning on it—mostly. And, in any case, Richard was only going to be gone for a week or so…although, Emily thought, by the time he returned Philip and Helen could very well be an established couple. Philip was, among other things, a fast worker.

She turned back to her computer screen and the email she'd been in the middle of composing, but the words danced before her eyes. All she could really see was Richard's defeated look, his disappointed smile, and she wondered if for once she'd interfered just a little too much.

CHAPTER SIX

EMILY pulled at the tight satin bodice of her brides-maid's dress and grimaced in the mirror. The hot pink colour made her look like a piece of bubblegum, and the skirt belled out around her knees so she was halfway to wearing a tutu. Stephanie, however, had been enamoured with what she thought was a fairy tale dress, and insisted Emily looked gorgeous in it. Emily silently disagreed with Stephanie's assessment, but offered no resistance. This was Stephanie's day, not hers.

The wedding was to be a small, intimate affair, the ceremony taking place in the church of the Hampshire village where Stephanie had grown up, and the reception a dinner at a local hotel afterwards. Emily had arrived last night just in time to make the rehearsal, and then fallen into bed, exhausted and a bit overwhelmed by the general pandemoni-um and near hysteria an imminent wedding caused. Seating plans. Bouquets. A last minute alteration to Stephanie's dress. Emily's head swam.

Since last night she'd only seen Stephanie and Tim

and their families and attendants, and she hadn't had time to ask Stephanie if Jason would be coming to the wedding.

No, that wasn't really true, Emily acknowledged to herself as she fixed her hair into what she hoped was a neat chignon. She'd had plenty of time to talk to Stephanie over the last two weeks. She hadn't *wanted* to ask about Jason because she didn't even want to think about him, or that kiss, and she certainly wasn't going to give her friend any reason to think there was something between her and Jason. Because there wasn't. How could there be? The thought was beyond ludicrous.

All they'd shared was a single kiss—a kiss that had been part punishment and part proof, as Jason had said himself. As if that kiss proved anything about Richard Marsden. Or even Jason. All right, it proved Jason was a decent kisser, but that was hardly relevant to anything. Or anyone. Certainly not to her.

And yet Emily could not quite forget the feel of Jason's lips on hers, how they'd been both hard and soft, warm and cool, and even more aggravatingly— and alarmingly—how she'd responded to that kiss, as if he'd lit a candle inside of her. Not just a candle, but a roaring fire. And it still hadn't gone out.

A knock sounded at the door of the spare bedroom in Stephanie's parents' house, where Emily had been getting ready.

'The car's here,' Joanne, Stephanie's mother, called. 'Are you all set, dear?'

'Yes…just about.' With a last rather despairing look at her tutu-like dress, Emily turned towards the door.

The ceremony was beautiful, just as Emily had known it would be. The church sanctuary was bedecked with ivy and white roses, and a hushed silence prevailed as Tim and Stephanie exchanged their vows, their voices ringing with heartfelt sincerity and love.

This was why people got married, Emily thought with an unfamiliar wrenching inside. She'd consider it herself if she ever met a man who would look at her the way Tim looked at Stephanie. Not with disapproval, or amusement, or—

She was thinking about Jason. Again. Emily forced the thoughts away and let her gaze wander around the church. There were a handful of people from work but, other than that, few she recognised. Then she heard a quiet creak as someone opened the door to the church and slipped into the last pew.

It took Emily a stunned second to process who it was.

Jason.

His gaze locked on hers and held it, refusing to look away, his eyes calm yet his jaw tense. He looked…*determined* was the only word for it, as if he had a goal in mind and he fully intended to achieve it. Perhaps that was the way he looked at a flooded river, or a swamped stream, or—

But, no. He was looking at her, and Emily could not look away. She couldn't move. It was as if Jason's gaze was actually trapping her, and her hands clenched around her posy of rosebuds, the dress cutting into her ribcage, her gaze locked on Jason's. Her gaze, of its own accord, moved to his mouth, took in those firm, sculpted lips. How had she never before noticed what amazing lips he had? They'd been on hers. Hard on hers.

One kiss. Just one kiss, and yet she couldn't forget it. She had a feeling she never would. She swallowed, her throat suddenly unbearably dry. Jason still gazed at her, steady, unyielding.

'And by the power invested in me, I now pronounce you man and wife.'

Finally, Emily possessed the ability to tear her gaze from Jason's and she clapped along with everyone else as Tim, beaming, took his wife in his arms. She watched as he kissed her, a kiss filled with passion and love and happiness. That kiss was a declaration, a celebration, a shout of joy to the world.

Jason hadn't kissed her like that. No one had.

Swallowing again, Emily glanced back at Jason. He was chatting with the person in front of him, oblivious to her now. Emily wondered if she'd actually imagined the intensity of the moment before; surely Jason hadn't been looking at her quite like that.

Like what? her mind mocked, for she didn't even know.

Stephanie and Tim had broken their kiss and were now beaming at everyone around them. Emily felt another wrench of what could only be envy. She'd meant what she'd said to Jason; she was happy, and she certainly didn't need anything. The search for the kind of love Stephanie and Tim shared was exhausting and uncertain, and she had no desire to embark on it only to end up frustrated and alone. Better to be happy and alone, surely.

Yet that didn't keep her from wanting for a moment—just a moment—what Stephanie and Tim had. She wanted it desperately. She longed for someone to look at her the way Tim had looked at Stephanie, with love, his face softened with adoration. She wanted to be desired, treasured, adored. Wined and dined and romanced. Swept off her feet.

It wasn't going to happen.

Determinedly, she shrugged the feeling aside. Surely it was no more than even the most hardened heart would feel at a wedding as lovely as this one. It would pass.

Smiling at her radiant friend, Emily followed them down the aisle. She made sure to keep her face averted as she passed the last pew.

Of course she couldn't avoid Jason for ever. She

tried to, and managed it through drinks and dinner. Her duty as bridesmaid kept her close to Stephanie's side, straightening her veil, fetching her a glass of water, smiling until her cheeks ached for the requisite round of photographs.

Yet when the dancing started and Stephanie and Tim took the floor, Jason headed directly to her and she realised she'd been waiting—and even expecting—him to. Emily's heart started a heavy thud of anticipation as she watched him stride across the ballroom, as purposeful and self-assured as always. His hair and eyes both glinted near-gold in the dim lighting and she could see the ripple of muscles under his immaculate suit, the easy shrug of his shoulders as he walked.

She wondered what he was going to say to her, if he would mention the kiss. Should she act unconcerned, indifferent, as if she'd already dismissed it as the nothing encounter it surely was—for him, at least? Yet that would be an act, and he would surely know it. He'd probably tease her about it, but at least then they would be on familiar footing.

Her palms grew slippery as she clutched her flute of champagne. She wished she'd reapplied her lipstick. She also wished she wasn't wearing a poufy, too-tight bridesmaid dress in shocking pink satin.

'Care to dance?'

The words shocked her, brought her back to the last wedding she'd attended with Jason, when he'd asked the same question and held his hand out in just the same way…and she'd been wearing pink satin then too. Some things never changed.

'Fine,' she said, realising that sounded a bit ungracious.

Jason, however, just smiled, although Emily saw his eyes didn't respond. They still held that same hard determination, and Emily wondered at its source.

She placed her hand in his, let his fingers enfold hers as he led her onto the small parquet dance floor. His other hand rested on her waist, warm and large, his fingers splaying across her hip.

The band was playing a low, lazy tune, something you only needed to sway to. Emily kept her gaze focused in the region of Jason's chin as they moved to the music. They were closer than six inches apart this time, and this was no boring waltz. She could feel the heat from his body, inhaled the tang of his aftershave. He was a good dancer, she realised with some surprise; he swayed well, his movements languorous, even sexy, his sure hands guiding her to his own lazy rhythm.

Emily could not look him in the face. She felt agonisingly aware of him, and also of the memory of dancing with him seven years ago. She'd been so affected and overwhelmed by him then. Clearly nothing had changed.

Jason touched her chin with his finger. 'Can't you look at me?'

Reluctantly, Emily forced her gaze upwards. 'Of

course.' Yet when she took in the blaze of his eyes, the wry twisting of his lips, she wished she hadn't risen to his challenge. She couldn't look at him. She couldn't tell what he felt. Or if he was thinking about their kiss the way she was…with every nerve and muscle of her body.

Involuntarily she'd stiffened, the memories and uncertainties causing her to stop their slow dance, and Jason gently nudged her hip with his hand, forcing her to move again. Sway. Her hip came into gentle contact with his and she felt a lightning shaft of awareness. Bone against bone. She angled her body away from his, which was difficult considering how close he was holding her.

'Are you acting so skittish because I kissed you?' he asked in that practical, matter-of-fact way that was so essentially Jason, and at this moment Emily did not know how to respond. All her witty retorts seemed to have evaporated. Banter was beyond her.

'Ah, yes, that kiss,' she finally said, her tone sounding cringingly false and even hearty. 'How could I forget?'

'It would be a poor reflection on me if you had forgotten,' Jason observed.

She risked a glance upwards; he was gazing at her with a steady, intense assessment that was more unnerving than any glower or scowl. He looked like he was trying to understand her, and surely she didn't want *that*. 'You mean on your kissing abilities?' she queried flippantly. Or at least as flippantly as she could.

'Quite. However,' Jason continued, pulling her closer again so their hips gently collided once more, sending a shaft of agonising awareness low through her pelvis, 'I know you didn't forget, and I'm in no doubt of my own abilities.'

Emily let out a little huffy laugh. 'That's a bit arrogant.'

'Is it?' Jason touched her chin with his thumb, angling her face upwards. His mouth was a whisper away from hers. 'You wanted me to kiss you seven years ago, Em. Things haven't changed that much, have they?'

'Actually, they have,' Emily retorted, her words sharpening. She did not want to be reminded of that night, not when Jason's kiss—and her own humiliating response—was so fresh and raw in her mind. Her heart. Things *had* changed; she was different. 'In any case, Jason, if you meant that kiss as some kind of proof, I'm sorry to say it failed.'

'Proof?' Jason repeated. He sounded genuinely puzzled. 'Proof of what?'

'That Richard's not boring,' Emily said impatiently. He'd told her so himself, so why was he looking at her as if she had just said something utterly nonsensical? 'You said,' she reminded him. 'Remember?'

In one quick yet fluid motion, Jason guided her off the dance floor. Emily could barely keep up with him, tripping in her heels, his hand now encircling her wrist, as he led her from the crowded ballroom to a small secluded lounge off the lobby of the hotel. The sudden silence unnerved her, left her defence-less. All she could hear was the ragged tear of her own breathing, and all the words that hadn't yet been said.

Jason stared at her for a long moment, spots of colour high on his cheekbones although his eyes were assessing and cool. 'What?' Emily demanded. 'You told me yourself, Jason.'

'I know I did,' he said, his voice as calm and measured as always despite the colour still flaring in his face, 'but only because you needed a reason.' A faint smile flickered over his features. 'As far as responses to a kiss go, "What was that for?" is fairly insulting.'

'But logical,' Emily returned. 'Why else would you kiss me, Jason?'

Jason's eyebrows rose. 'Why *else*?'

'You never wanted to before.'

He kept staring at her, his brow furrowed now as if he were figuring out a complicated maths problem... or her. Emily crossed her arms over her chest, the pink satin stretching alarmingly across her breasts. She was really beginning to regret this dress.

'Is this about the time we danced at Isobel and Jack's wedding? All those years ago? How I sup-posedly humiliated you?'

He sounded so disbelieving that Emily knew he

didn't know. Hadn't seen how she'd bolted from the dance floor in tears. Although it amazed her that he hadn't noticed; she'd felt so obvious and exposed. 'It was a long time ago, I know,' she said stiffly. 'And of course it hardly matters now—'

'Of course it does matter,' Jason cut across her, 'since we're having this conversation.'

'I just felt very rejected,' Emily said, her words stilted and stiff, each one drawn from her with the utmost reluctance. She had wanted to banish this memory, had convinced herself she had. Yet seeing Jason again—having him mention it after so many years of silence—brought it all rushing back, made her realise afresh how painful that little episode had been. She couldn't laugh about it now; maybe she never had been able to.

And now she felt as if she were giving Jason more ammunition to tease her, or at least give her one of those coolly mocking looks. She waited for one eyebrow to arch as he gave her some dry rejoinder. *If you're going to offer yourself on a plate, Em…*

Instead, he said something else entirely. 'Emily, I told you then how I wanted to kiss you.'

She stared at him, shocked, totally unprepared for this admission. 'No, you didn't—'

'Yes, I did,' Jason replied, his words sharp, as if he were angry about the truth of it. As if he hadn't wanted to want to kiss her. Perhaps he hadn't. 'In fact, I remember exactly what I said. You asked if I'd like to kiss you, and I told you I would, *rather.*'

'But I won't,' Emily finished woodenly.

Jason stared at her for another endless moment before the corner of his mouth quirked upwards. 'And clearly you only paid attention to the second clause of that sentence.'

'And clearly you aced grammar,' Emily threw back at him. She didn't want to talk about this any more; she didn't want to remember. 'Look, it really doesn't matter. It was seven years ago.' She let out a long breath that shuddered only slightly. 'It was just a moment. A silly moment.' Why had she ever asked him to kiss her? And why hadn't she been able to forget when he finally had?

'It wasn't,' Jason said quietly, 'a silly moment for me.'

Emily froze. Forgot to breathe. She could not make sense of his words; they fell into the taut stillness between them and lay there, demanding she do something with them. *Ask.* 'What are you talking about?' she finally whispered.

'I wanted to kiss you, Emily,' Jason said. His voice was quiet and yet so very matter-of-fact. 'I wanted to kiss you very badly, but I didn't because you were seventeen years old and I doubted you'd ever been kissed before.'

Colour washed her cheekbones. 'I hadn't,' she admitted, her voice still no more than a thread of sound.

'I was twenty-nine. Older than you are now. And the realisation that I could want to kiss you, want *you* so much terrified and shamed me. You were too young.'

Emily stared at him as she tested the truth of his words. She remembered how he'd glared at her; he'd looked so angry. 'But you…you pushed me away like you couldn't stand the thought of me—or kissing me!' she finally burst out, amazed that it could hurt even now. For years she'd convinced herself that silly little moment between them had been nothing more than that. Silly. Little. Yet now she knew she couldn't pretend, not when Jason was being so honest. That silly little moment hadn't been silly—or little—at all. Not for her, and perhaps not even for Jason.

'I pushed you away,' Jason said, his patience clearly starting to fray, 'because I didn't want to humiliate myself—or you! There couldn't be anything between us then, not when you were no more than a teenager.'

Then. He made it sound as if it might be different now. As if something—what?—could happen between them now. The thought was so overwhelming, so alarming and exciting and yet somehow preposterous, that Emily could think of nothing to say. She didn't even know how she felt, how to untangle this confusing rush of emotions—shock, fear, anxiety, excitement, hope—that raced dizzily through her and left her robbed of speech or even breath, so she could only stare at him, helpless, hopeful, waiting.

* * *

Jason watched several different emotions chase themselves across Emily's features. He'd shocked her, he knew. He'd been honest—more honest than he'd intended—and now she didn't know what to say. Think. Feel.

And neither did he. His mind and body had been in a ferment for too long. He couldn't keep himself from Emily, despite every intention to do just that. Time and time again he'd sought her out, been drawn to her in a way he could not resist. The realisation was aggravating. Humbling too. He'd always prided himself on his sense of self-control, his iron resolve—both had crumbled to nothing when he'd finally given into desire and kissed Emily, felt her sweet, yielding response, her lips parting under his, her body curving against him. He wanted Emily. He'd gone to Africa to escape her, escape the attraction he'd felt, and instead he'd endured days of remembering just how she'd felt and tasted, nights where he'd relived that one kiss in his mind. And imagined a few other things besides.

Even work hadn't been enough of a distraction, and after a week of it he'd realised what he wanted. What he needed.

To get Emily out of his system. And the only way to do that, to move forward, was to have her. In his arms, in his bed.

Why not?

She'd told him she wasn't interested in love. Not for herself at any rate. She wanted to have fun. She'd had several relationships already and was wise to the ways of the world. So why shouldn't they indulge in what would be a very basic and pleasurable affair? She wasn't seventeen any more. She wasn't innocent any more.

He'd been afraid of hurting her back then, of course he had. But Emily had already shown him how unimpressed she was with him already—she thought he was *boring*, out of bed at least; Jason saw the positive side of that assessment now. It meant she wasn't in love with him. She didn't want to marry him.

But she wanted him. He knew that. And as long as he didn't hurt or disappoint her—which he wouldn't, since her heart wasn't involved—why shouldn't they enjoy themselves? It had suddenly seemed wonderfully simple. And easy.

Although from the way Emily was looking at him now, with so much dazed uncertainty, Jason knew it didn't seem so simple to her. She hadn't believed he desired her. The thought was laughable; it seemed so glaringly—and painfully—obvious to him. Clearly, Emily had her doubts.

He looked forward to removing them. And a few other things, as well.

'What…' she began, her voice scratchy. Her tongue darted out to moisten her lips. Jason's gut clenched. 'What are you saying?'

Jason let his gaze rest on her, his eyes heavy-lidded, his expression thoughtful. Suggestive. He saw

Emily's eyes widen, her pupils dilate. 'Things have changed,' he said finally, his voice no more than a steady, low thrum. He took a step closer to her, lifted his hand to touch her chin, his thumb grazing her jawbone. He felt her response shudder through her. 'Haven't they?' Her lips parted, but no words came out. Jason smiled and lowered his head, his lips a breath away from hers. He could feel her tremble, sway towards him. 'Not too much, though…' He waited, his mouth hovering over hers, needing her response. Her acceptance. She needed to understand what he was saying… and what he wasn't.

'Jason…'

'Emily?'

Emily jerked away from him as Stephanie's sister-in-law Lucy, terrifyingly organised and brisk, popped her head in the little lounge. 'There you are! Stephanie is about to throw her bouquet. You won't want to miss it.'

Jason watched as Emily's face flooded with colour. She turned away from him, her head clearly averted from his gaze. 'Thank you, Lucy. I'll be right there.'

Lucy disappeared and still Emily hesitated for a moment, her back to Jason, clearly waiting.

'We'll have to finish this…conversation…another time,' he said. He took a breath and let it out slowly, needing to state the obvious. Wanting her to understand. 'I want you, Emily. But I don't want you to be hurt.' He waited, willing her to agree, to say something at least, to indicate she understood. *This is just a fling. Fun. What we both want.*

She half-turned so her face was in profile, and he saw the smooth curve of her cheek, the downward sweep of her golden lashes. She looked uncertain and so very young. 'I won't get hurt,' she said, her voice low.

Yet as she slipped from the room Jason wondered if she'd spoken to convince him…or herself.

CHAPTER SEVEN

EMILY did not see Jason for a week. It was a week of anxiety and also a little anger, of tensing and turning every time someone came to her door, of wondering why he'd made such a startling confession and then disappeared without a trace.

Was he teasing her? Had he changed his mind? Or was he serious, and he was giving her time to decide what she wanted?

Emily didn't know which she preferred. Every option seemed alarming. Meanwhile, she found she was checking her mobile for messages or texts far too often. She scoured the internet's social networking pages to see if he was on any, which of course he wasn't. Jason was hardly the kind of man to update his online status. Annoyed with herself, she stayed away from her mobile and laptop except for work, determined not to think of him at all.

Unfortunately, that proved impossible. She kept going over her conversation with Jason again and again, marvelling at his words...and their meaning.

I want you, Emily. But I don't want you to be hurt.

It amazed her to think that Jason desired her now, had been intimating that he wanted there to be something between them now.

But what? A kiss? A fling? Clearly, he wasn't proposing marriage, and that was the last thing she wanted anyway. She wasn't in love with Jason; she wasn't in love with anyone. But she wanted him. And he wanted her.

It could be so very simple. She wouldn't get hurt, just as she'd told him. So why was she still mired in doubt?

Perhaps, Emily reflected, it was because it seemed so *impossible* for Jason to want her physically. And even for her to want him. They had so much history, so many shared memories and moments that were at odds with what he was feeling now. What she was feeling.

If she were honest, the thought of Jason actually desiring her terrified and excited her in equal amounts. She'd *never* thought of him that way, never dared to…and yet another part of her sly mind whispered that in reality she'd *always* thought of him that way, or wanted to. That was why that dance—and almost-kiss—seven years ago had actually devastated her…even though she'd convinced herself for so long that it hadn't. That it had been nothing.

And now? Emily didn't know what the truth was, or could be. She was afraid to find out. Maybe Jason hadn't meant that at all anyway. Perhaps he'd just been teasing her as usual, and she'd read far too much into a few throwaway remarks because her own need was suddenly so great. Maybe she was making everything up in her mind, and the next time she saw Jason he would be back to his familiar, mocking self, one eyebrow arched, a faint smile curving his mouth.

Oh, that mouth…

She really was a mess. An obsessed mess, she acknowledged as she kept checking her phone and surfing the Internet and looking for clues to the truth about Jason because he wasn't there in person. Even if he had been she knew she did not yet possess the courage to confront him about any of it.

Meanwhile November drifted into December, and the charity fund-raiser at Jason's flat loomed closer. Emily could barely hide her surprise when Gillian Bateson approached her again, for help with the organisation.

'I thought you had it well in hand?' she asked, surveying Gillian from across her desk. The older woman looked a little more subdued than usual. Her hair was not as immaculately styled and her nail varnish was chipped. Her smile seemed a bit fixed.

'Oh, I do, of course I do. But I thought you might like a peek at Jason's penthouse. It's fab, you know—or actually you don't—'

Emily gritted her teeth. 'I'm sure it is, and I'll see it at the party. I don't really need a…a peek.' Even if she was intensely curious about where Jason lived. Where Jason slept.

Gillian paused, her gaze sliding away from Emily's. 'Actually, I could use a little help,' she said, the admission drawn from her with obvious reluctance. 'It turns out my daughter is visiting that weekend, and I promised to take her out for a bit—' She glanced back at Emily, her laugh a little wobbly. 'You have no idea how demanding pre-teens are.'

'I can imagine, considering I was one myself once.' Emily smiled, surprised and gratified by this insight into Gillian's life. She knew it was practically killing her to ask for help, but Emily was glad she had. And she was honest enough to admit to herself she did want a peek at Jason's flat—badly. 'I'd be happy to help, Gillian.'

After Gillian left her office Emily stared at her computer screen, restless yet needing to work. She had not been able to concentrate on anything. Her fingers drummed on her desktop and she glanced at her to-do list scribbled on a spare piece of paper. She was meant to follow up a shortlist of applications for an assistant in the legal department, arrange the details for an expatriate hire, and draft an email regarding intra-office communications. And that was just this morning. Sighing, she reached for her empty coffee mug.

She was just about to stagger to the coffee machine when her mobile rang. She glanced at the number; it was Philip.

'Hello, sweetheart,' he practically purred. 'Heading out to any Christmas parties this weekend?'

Emily thought of the unanswered invitations scattered across her mantelpiece. 'I don't think so, Philip.'

'I've got two tickets to a new art exhibit in Soho,' Philip told her. 'Very exclusive. You free?'

A ripple of unease made its way down Emily's spine. Why was Philip inviting *her*? 'I don't think so, Philip. I'm quite busy this weekend.' She let out a little gasp, as if she'd just thought of something wonderful. 'I know. Why don't you ask Helen? You've been seeing a lot of her lately, haven't you?'

'I don't know whether I'd say a lot,' Philip replied, his tone one of bored dismissal. Emily froze, her fingers clenched around her mobile. This was not how Philip was meant to talk about Helen. Yet despite the icy feeling of dread developing in the pit of her stomach, she could not give up so easily.

'Well,' she said brightly, 'I'm sure she'd love to go to an art exhibit…and you two were certainly cosy when we all went out to the theatre…' She let out a little suggestive laugh, waiting for Philip's affirmation, but instead he just gave a rather dry chuckle.

'Only because you dragged her along.'

Emily nearly dropped her phone. 'But…but Philip!' she said, her voice rising to something between a squeak and a shriek. 'You were so… you sat next to her…you touched her hair…' She sounded ridiculous, Emily thought distantly, but surely she couldn't have been so terribly mistaken. So *wrong*.

'You thought I was interested in *Helen*?' Philip asked, and then laughed. There was nothing funny about that laugh, nothing warm or generous. It was a laugh of scorn, of mockery. It made Emily's insides shrivel. 'Come on, Emily. She's a lovely girl, of course, but...' He sounded horribly patronising.

'But?' Emily prompted coldly.

'Well, she's not our sort, is she?' Philip said, and Emily could tell he was trying to be reasonable. 'I thought you were dragging her around as some sort of charity case, and I was nice enough to her because of that, but you couldn't actually think...' He laughed again, and Emily closed her eyes.

Oh, no. No, no, *no*. This was not how she'd imagined this conversation going at all. Philip was supposed to start gushing about Helen, and how lucky he was, and Emily had even envisioned a little teary-eyed gratitude towards the person who had pushed them together. *Push* being the operative word.

This was bad. This was very, very bad for Helen, and almost as bad for her because it meant she'd been horribly, humiliatingly wrong.

And Jason had been right.

Both realisations were equally painful. She opened her eyes and took a deep breath. 'Then I think you've been a bit unfair to Helen,' she said, her voice tight with both anger and guilt. 'You've certainly spent enough time with her so she might think—'

'You're the one who seems to think something,' Philip cut her off. 'Not Helen.'

There was too much truth in that statement for Emily to object. She *had* encouraged Helen. If she'd given her a word of caution instead, who knew how much of this mess might have been averted. And, Emily was forced to acknowledge miserably, she'd encouraged Helen at least in part because it had been a way of proving something to Jason. Of showing him he was wrong.

Except it looked like he wasn't.

'Well, I'm afraid I'm not free this weekend, Philip,' Emily said, her voice decidedly frosty. 'Goodbye.'

She disconnected the call and then with a groan buried her head in her hands. Shame and regret roiled through her. She heard Helen asking her, *Do you think he likes me?* and her own assured— smug!—response: *I'm sure of it.*

And now…now she would have to tell Helen just how awful Philip was. She surely could not let Helen go on wondering, *hoping*…yet how could she do it? How could she admit how wrong she'd been? Wrong on one occasion, at least.

She straightened in her chair. She might have been wrong about Philip, but she was still right about Richard. He was the same, just as she'd always known.

Predictable. Steady. Cautious. And far too sensible.

Just like—

Emily stopped that train of thought immediately. It wasn't going anywhere good. And, really, she needed to focus on Helen, who deserved someone special, someone who would sweep her off her feet properly—

Already she began a mental flip through the eligible men she knew. Doug in accounting was divorced; Eric, a friend of a friend was reportedly single although there had been rumours of—

She forced herself to stop. It was too soon to set Helen up with someone else and, considering this current catastrophe, perhaps she should take a short break from matchmaking. Relationships could so clearly be disastrous.

At lunchtime Emily went reluctantly downstairs, knowing she would see Helen and somehow have to break the news.

Helen's face lit up as Emily entered the lobby. Emily forced herself to smile back. 'Are you free? I thought we could grab a bite.'

Helen nodded happily. 'Oh, yes—' Then she gave herself away by glancing towards the blank screen of her mobile; Emily had a sinking feeling she'd been waiting for Philip to ring.

'Come on, then,' she said in an attempt at brisk cheer, and hurried Helen out of the building.

In the end the only way to tell Helen was honestly, flatly, without any evasions. Emily kept it as brief as possible, not wanting Helen even to guess at Philip's awful attitude of contempt.

'I'm sorry, Helen,' she said after she'd told her, in the kindest terms possible, about Philip's decided lack of interest. 'I know it's my fault for encouraging you—I really thought he was a better man than he is. And—' she swallowed, forcing herself to meet Helen's bewildered, wide-eyed gaze '—and honestly I think you're better off without him. I just wish I'd realised that a bit sooner.'

Helen glanced down at her untouched lunch. 'You can hardly blame yourself,' she said quietly. 'I'm a grown woman, Emily, and I was the one who—' She swallowed and sniffed, making Emily's heart ache again with guilt and regret. 'And I let myself be blinded by him. He was so charming, and when he…we…' She stopped, sniffing again, and a wave of dread crashed over Emily.

'Helen…did anything actually…*happen* between the two of you?'

Miserably, Helen nodded. 'A few weeks ago, after the theatre, I…I invited him back afterwards. I didn't tell you because I didn't want you to think I was… well…' She stopped as tears began to silently leak out of the corners of her eyes. 'You're so together, Emily, and everyone likes you even if you don't need anyone. But I was lonely and he seemed so nice—'

Emily reached across the table and clasped Helen's hand tightly. She felt perilously close to tears herself. 'This is all my fault,' she said quietly, guilt lancing through her again, causing a physical pain. 'All my fault.' Damn Philip. He might have been quick to dismiss Helen to her that morning, but he'd obviously liked her enough to take her to bed. The thought made Emily's insides burn with both shame and anger. The blame could not be laid solely at Philip's feet. The man was a snake, but she'd convinced Helen he was kind and charming. She'd convinced herself, as well. The only person she hadn't convinced was Jason. 'I'm so sorry, Helen,' she said uselessly, for the damage was already done. This was why she kept herself out of relationships. Perhaps she should start keeping other people out of them too.

Her matchmaking days, Emily thought grimly, were over.

The next few days passed in a blur of work and regret. Emily could not let go of the guilt that ate at her for pushing Helen towards Philip. She dreaded seeing Jason, knowing he'd been right all along and would undoubtedly let her know it too, yet he didn't make an appearance.

'He had to fly back to Africa again for a few days,' Eloise told her when Emily broke down and asked for information. 'But he'll be back for the fund-raiser.'

The charity fund-raiser, next week at his flat. Emily would be going early to help decorate, and yet while this thought had filled her with a certain tense expectation just a few days ago, now it was accompanied by a different dread. She wasn't really looking forward to admitting he'd been right, which, knowing Jason, she would be forced to do sooner or later. She certainly wasn't looking forward to his response.

What did I tell you, Em? Sensible is what women need...

No, it isn't, she thought crossly. It *isn't*.

Still, curiosity and anticipation helped to staunch that deepening dread as she headed over to Jason's flat in Chelsea Harbour that Friday afternoon. She'd invited Helen as her guest, hoping an evening out—without Philip in attendance—would help cheer her up. She tried not to think of what Jason might say about that; no doubt he would accuse her of meddling again.

The air was sharp with cold as she and Helen climbed into a cab and headed for the well-heeled neighbourhood just north of the Thames.

Gillian had given her a detailed list of instructions about the caterers, the decorators and the musicians. All Emily would have to do was supervise. And perhaps have a *little* peek round.

A tingle of excitement made its way up her spine as she and Helen left the cab for the sleek modern building that housed Jason's penthouse. The high-speed lift had her racing to the top floor, and the doors swished silently open directly into Jason's flat. His home.

Emily stepped gingerly onto a floor of highly polished ebony that seemed to stretch endlessly in several directions. The flat was as fabulous as Gillian had said, and also stark. And even soulless. If she'd been hoping to gain some clue into Jason's inner workings—or even his heart—from where he lived, then she was surely disappointed. The flat revealed nothing. Perhaps, Emily thought wryly, that was indicative of his inner workings. Jason was not a man given to great emotion.

Emily stepped into a soaring reception room with floor-to-ceiling windows overlooking the river. Just as Gillian had said, everything was black or white. Or black and white. Emily took in several very expensive looking black leather sofas, a coffee table of white marble that looked like a piece of modern sculpture, a canvas hanging over the black marble fireplace that was nothing more than a rectangle of white with one messy splotch of black ink in the bottom right corner. It had probably sold for thousands of pounds, Emily thought wryly, and it looked like something her niece had made by accident.

She glanced in the dining room and took in the huge ebony table and matching chairs, a thick snowy-white carpet and several more modern canvases—one black-and-white prison stripes, another like the stripes of a zebra. It was amazing. It was awful.

It revealed nothing about Jason, not the Jason she knew, the man who had always been there to bail her out and scold her afterwards, who managed to smile with both disapproval and amusement, whose eyes turned the colour of honey—

The man who had kissed her. And who had *wanted* to kiss her, maybe more than once.

The buzzer sounded and Emily jumped nearly a foot in the air. The caterers must have arrived. She and Helen exchanged guilty looks—they'd both been snooping—and Emily went to let them in.

The next hour was spent organising all the staff, checking on a thousand tiny details and dealing with the dozens of texts from Gillian, who still clearly wanted to have a hand in the operations.

'I thought you were at a film,' Emily said when Gillian rang her for the third time.

'I am,' Gillian told her. 'Some boy band thing. It's dire. Did the caterers find white asparagus?'

'Yes, and black truffles.' Even the canapés were black and white. 'Don't worry, Gillian. Just enjoy your time with your daughter.'

Gillian let out a rather trembling sigh. 'It's just so odd,' she confessed in a low voice. 'We haven't spent much time together at all.'

Emily's heart twisted in more sympathy than she'd ever had for Gillian before. 'Then go spend some,' she said, 'boy band film and all.'

Finally, by half past six, almost everything was set up. Emily glanced at the makeshift bar, the string quartet, the caterers, and let out a breathy sigh of relief. She hadn't realised how much organisation a party like this actually took.

'Everything looks wonderful,' Helen said, and Emily gave her a grateful smile.

'Gillian said we could use the guest suites to shower and change—shall we get cleaned up?'

Helen nodded and, after grabbing their bags they headed down the long corridor—stark white walls and ebony flooring—towards the bedroom wing. Gillian had told her the guest rooms were the first two doors and, after Helen had disappeared into the first room, an irrepressible curiosity made Emily tiptoe towards the third and last door. Jason's bedroom.

Her heart began to thud as she gently pushed open the door and stepped into the room. Her feet sank into the plush white carpet and she gazed at the king-sized bed with its black satin sheets. Although the sheets were drawn across the wide bed with military precision, she pictured them pulled back and rumpled, with Jason lying there—naked.

Good heavens. Where had that thought come from? It had sprung into her mind so suddenly, so vividly, that her cheeks burned and she glanced around guiltily. Still, she could imagine it all too easily and yet not at all, because nothing about this bed or room or entire flat made her think of Jason. And of course she'd never seen him naked. And most likely never would—

'I think you've wandered into the wrong bedroom.' *Oh!* Emily whirled around, one hand to her thumping heart. Jason stood in the doorway, his shoulder propped against the frame, one hand already starting to loosen his tie. His eyes glinted with humour and his mouth quirked upwards. 'Haven't you?' he added so Emily's face burned all the more and she could feel herself going scarlet. Lovely. Just the look she was going for.

She arched an eyebrow, tossing her hair over her shoulder. 'I was just checking to see if there's any colour in this place,' she said, striving to sound nonchalant. 'I have this mad urge to spill a can of red paint on your carpet.'

'That sounds interesting,' Jason said. 'Although my decorator would have a fit. I suppose I can start with this.' Emily watched in a sort of horrified fascination as Jason tugged off his tie—red silk—and tossed it onto a nearby chair. It landed on the white suede like a splash of paint. Emily swallowed.

'That's a start,' she managed with a light little laugh. 'Although this place still is rather stark.' She gave him a teasing smile, the kind of smile she'd always given him, except now it felt like flirting. And, even stranger still, it felt like Jason was flirting back, an answering smile quirking the corners of his mouth—*those lips*—as he held her gaze a second longer than necessary. A second full of heat. She hadn't imagined what he'd said at Stephanie's wedding. What he'd wanted.

Emily cleared her throat. 'I apologise for being so curious,' she said after a few seconds as Jason simply gazed at her, his eyes sweeping over her rather dishevelled state, lingering on...certain places. Making her feel hot and shivery all at once. 'Anyway,' she said, struggling for words, for air, 'I just couldn't imagine you living in a place like this.'

'I don't live here very much, to tell you the truth,' Jason replied. He dropped his attaché case by the bed and then shrugged out of his suit jacket, dropping it onto the same chair as the tie.

Emily watched his muscles ripple under the crisp white cotton. She'd never quite realised how *built* Jason was. Did he work out? Or did he just lift things when he was doing all that engineering stuff? She swallowed again and tore her gaze away from him. She had to get a grip on this conversation—or at least herself. 'Now that you're back for a bit perhaps you should invest in a new decorator.'

Jason chuckled. His fingers went to the buttons of his shirt. Was he actually undressing? Was he going to take his shirt *off*? Emily found she couldn't breathe. She was staring at his hands as they slid the first button out of its hole and she caught a glimpse of the strong brown column of his throat.

'I suppose I'll never think of this place as home,' Jason said musingly. He seemed unaware that he was undressing in front of her, or that she was staring. 'Weldon will always be that.'

Weldon, Jason's family estate, sprawling and comfortable, one of Surrey's finest homes, yet he hadn't been there properly in years. 'Do you think you'll move back there one day?' she asked.

He paused, his fingers stilling on the buttons of his shirt. Her mesmerised stare finally broken, Emily lifted her gaze to Jason's face. He was watching her with that same little knowing smile. Not so unaware, then. He knew he was unnerving her; he was teasing her. Like always. Except…not.

'Yes, eventually. I'll need to take care of the estate.' A slight frown had settled between his brows, even as he undid another button.

Emily swallowed. 'Yes…to produce that heir of yours, I suppose. Find any suitable candidates yet?' The words held a bit of an edge, but her gaze was still hopelessly drawn to Jason's shirt and how he was slowly—so slowly—unbuttoning it.

'Actually, no,' he said. 'Not yet.'

And not her. The thought really shouldn't bother her, Emily told herself almost frantically. She surely did not want to be in the running for that rather tedious role. And whatever was—or could be—between her and Jason, it certainly wasn't marriage. Or love.

Just basic, primal, overwhelming attraction.

Jason's fingers moved lower. If he undid another button, Emily thought with a lurch of panic, she'd be able to see his chest. 'But I'm not really looking at the moment,' he added. His fingers hovered over the button and Emily realised she was staring. Again. And Jason knew it. Even though her whole body felt heavy and strange, as if it belonged to someone else, she managed a step towards the door.

'Well, I suppose I should get dressed,' she said, attempting a brisk tone. Her voice wobbled instead. 'So I'll leave you to it...' She gestured towards his state of half-undress, her face reddening once more. She could *feel* the heat coming off her. And from Jason. It was all so new, so overwhelming, she felt as if her brain had been short-circuited All she could do was feel. *Want.*

'Don't rush off on my account,' Jason replied, his words laced with lazy amusement. 'You obviously wanted to be in my bedroom, Em...'

Emily froze. 'I was just looking,' she said stiffly.

'And you still are,' Jason replied softly. He'd undone that third button and once more Emily's gaze was glued to his chest. She knew it, he knew it, and yet she still couldn't move. That enticing glimpse of hard, sleek muscle and warm brown skin was making her remember how his chest had felt when she'd touched it—by accident—and how she would like to touch it again. Minus the shirt. What would his skin feel like? Warm, cool? Smooth, rough?

'Really, Jason,' she managed, finally tearing her gaze away from his chest. It took her a moment to focus on his face. 'I had no idea you were such a tease.'

'I'm not,' he told her, his voice low, and he took a step towards her.

Involuntarily, Emily took a step back. 'What are you doing?' she whispered.

Jason gazed at her for a moment, the glint of amusement gone from his eyes. His mouth thinned as he gave a little shake of his head. 'Terrifying you, apparently—'

'No—' Yet she could not deny the wild beat of her heart, the flush of her face. It wasn't terrifying, but it was something close. She certainly *felt*. A lot. And it scared her, even as desire raced through her veins, made her dizzy with need.

She wanted this. She wanted Jason. And yet she was afraid, because at least part of her knew that Jason was different, that she would be different with him. Everything would be different, deeper. Dangerous.

'Go get dressed, Em,' Jason said, turning away from her. He sounded tired. 'In another bedroom.'

Emily hesitated, wanting to say something witty and sophisticated. Something sexy. Yet she couldn't; her brain had frozen. Why did she still have to act so gauche with him?

Because this is Jason and you still feel like you're silly and giddy and seventeen years old.

'Fine,' she whispered and left the room, but not without looking back once, her gaze arrested as she watched Jason shrug out of his shirt, the bronzed muscles of his back rippling with the simple move-ment. Then his hands went to his belt buckle and she fled.

CHAPTER EIGHT

EMILY watched Jason from the other side of his living room, a glass of wine clutched in her hand. He looked breathtaking in a tuxedo, the elegant cut of his clothing emphasising his powerful frame, the breadth of his shoulders and the trimness of his hips. She hadn't really noticed either of those attributes before. She took a large gulp of wine.

Yet she *had* seen him in a tuxedo before. He'd worn one at Isobel's wedding. Perhaps that was why she'd asked him to kiss her. A man in a tuxedo was hard to resist. Jason was proving hard to resist.

Now that she'd acknowledged just how attracted she was to him, it seemed to be all she could think about. It certainly was all she could feel. And she wondered what could happen—tonight, even—if she let it.

She glanced over to where he stood, leaning against one of the living room's soaring white pillars. Her gaze remained fixed on the column of his throat and she imagined him undoing that little black bow tie, just like he'd undone his shirt buttons, revealing the warm skin underneath... She had a thing about his neck, apparently. And a few other parts of his body.

And Jason seemed to be thinking the same way about her. The thought caused an icy thrill to race down her spine right out to her fingers and toes. Icy and yet warm at the same time. Hot.

Perhaps she was coming down with a cold.

No, her fever was of an entirely different sort. And if Jason desired her—if he *suggested* something, how was she going to respond? It all seemed too incredible, too impossible. Any moment he would turn to her with a little smile, a shake of his head, and cluck his tongue.

Oh, Em...you didn't actually think...

She could, quite possibly, make a complete and utter ass of herself. She had to be careful. But then she'd always been rather careful in matters of the heart. Her heart, anyway. She'd been impulsive enough with Helen's.

Although Jason hadn't indicated any interest in her heart, of course. Love was out of the question, and he'd told her he didn't see her as a suitable candidate for marriage. Not that she was interested. No, this attraction between them was purely physical.

Her gaze returned yet again to Jason; he wasn't even looking at her. He hadn't looked at her all evening, and the realisation made her just a little bit annoyed. She was quite sure he was ignoring her—teasing her—on purpose. Sighing, she glanced around the room, checking that everyone was enjoying themselves—although not too much—and her heart sank a little bit when she saw Helen standing by the window, looking lost and forlorn. Emily realised with a little pang of guilt that she'd been so caught up in her lustful thoughts of Jason that she'd completely forgotten about Helen.

'Everything all right?' Stephanie came to stand beside her, her arm around her husband's waist. As former Head of HR, Stephanie was still on the guest list for the exclusive event. She and Tim had returned from their honeymoon only a week ago, and both still had that rapturous glow that made Emily feel both happy and sad—and a bit envious—at the same time. She'd never felt like that, not even close, and although there was nothing precisely missing from her life, standing next to her friend so radiant with joy, made her feel just a little...*less than*. Like something—or someone—was missing, and she didn't know what—or who—it was.

Was it Jason?

The question popped so suddenly and slyly into her head that Emily's mind blanked. How could she have even thought such a thing? What did that even *mean*? 'Sorry...' She turned to Stephanie, blinking as if she could clear the thought from her still-spinning mind. 'What did you say?'

Stephanie laughed. 'I just asked how things were... You look a million miles away, Emily!'

'Yes,' Emily admitted. She glanced again at

Helen, who still stood alone. Stephanie naturally followed her gaze.

'She looks rather lost, doesn't she?' she murmured.

'Yes.' Emily shifted uncomfortably. Perhaps inviting Helen to an event like this had been a mistake. Her friendship with Helen had seemed somewhat strained since Philip's about-face; she didn't know if it was out of her own sense of guilt or Helen's hurt. Probably both. 'I should go and talk to her,' she said, and excusing herself, started towards Helen, only to be waylaid by Gillian.

'We've run out of wine glasses,' she hissed. 'Stupid caterers didn't bring enough. I can't ask Jason—'

'I'll sort it out,' Emily soothed. Gillian had been on edge ever since she'd arrived, and Emily assumed it had to do with her daughter's visit. 'I'm sure we can borrow some.' She glanced again at Helen, who was looking more miserable by the minute.

'People are waiting for their wine…' Gillian bit her lip and Emily realised just how distressed she was. Gillian swiped angrily at her eyes. 'I'm sorry, I'm a mess. My daughter—'

'It's okay,' Emily said, squeezing her shoulder. 'I'll deal with it.'

It didn't take more than a few minutes to organise the glasses, and the crowd by the bar gratefully dispersed with drinks in hand. Emily turned to see to Helen and froze in horror. Stephanie had taken the matter into her own hands and was attempting to introduce Helen to the people standing near her. And one of them was Philip Ellsworth.

By the way a sleek blonde was clinging to him, Emily guessed he'd come as her date. She started towards them, wanting to intercede, yet she knew she wasn't in time. She could already hear Stephanie's cheerful voice.

'This is Sylvie, who volunteered for a well-building project last year, didn't you, Sylvie?'

The blonde nodded, and Emily had to grudgingly concede that, while she clearly had awful taste in men, she did possess an admirable altruistic streak. 'And this is...' Stephanie glanced at Philip, eyebrows raised enquiringly, and Emily watched with a sinking heart as he smiled rather smugly at Helen.

'Helen knows who I am,' he said, and there was enough innuendo in his voice to make Emily cringe. Stephanie looked confused and Helen bit her lip, her eyes filling with tears. She didn't say anything.

Damn Philip Ellsworth, Emily thought with a savage bitterness. She started forward, determined to rescue Helen, but someone else got there first.

'Helen.'

Emily's head jerked around as she heard Jason speak in a tone she almost didn't recognise. It was friendly and warm and intimate, and he crossed the room in a few long strides, placing his hand firmly on Helen's elbow as he smiled down at her. 'I don't think you've seen the view from the terrace. It's really quite stunning. The lights of the marina are spectacular at night.'

Emily watched as he expertly guided Helen away from the crowd—how many people had heard Philip's remark, guessed at his sly innuendo? Too many, Emily knew. Far too many. Yet now Helen smiled up at Jason as if he'd just charged in on his steed, and she allowed him to guide her outside.

And despite the guilt and regret that still lanced her, she felt a deep and heartfelt gratitude towards Jason for rescuing Helen. He might be a bit staid, a bit taciturn, but he was *kind*. Emily swallowed past the sudden lump of emotion in her throat. She had the uncomfortable feeling that she'd dismissed Jason all these years in a way perhaps she never should have. And it made her physical response to him all the more powerful—and alarming.

The party lasted until midnight. Emily could not focus enough to enjoy it, despite her best intentions to act as if she were. She chatted and smiled and laughed and pretended not to notice that Jason did not talk to her once the entire evening.

A month ago it wouldn't have mattered. A year ago it hadn't. Yet now everything had changed, *she* had changed, and this restless ache inside her would not go away. An ache for Jason. And though he didn't talk or even look at her the entire evening, she couldn't keep a sense of fizzy anticipation at bay, as intoxicating as the champagne she drank, filling her with bubbles of expectation. Surely Jason would seek her out before the end of the party. Surely *something* would happen.

Her mind left the details provocatively blank, although her body had no trouble remembering the slide of Jason's lips on hers, their urgent demand... and her unquestioning response.

As the guests filtered away, Emily organised the clearing up, the caterers and quartet packing up their supplies while Gillian tallied the amounts pledged towards the desalination plant. 'I think Jason will be very pleased,' she said smugly.

'Pleased about what?' Jason strolled into the living room, having seen the last of the guests off.

'Oh, Jason, you startled me.' Gillian fluttered her false eyelashes at him and all the goodwill Emily had been feeling towards her abruptly evaporated. 'We did very well tonight,' she continued, ever so slightly emphasising the *we*. 'Of course we'll have to wait until the cheques clear—'

'Wonderful,' Jason cut across her in a way Emily was quite familiar with. 'Now, Gillian, you look exhausted. I've called you a taxi,' he told her as Gillian's mouth dropped open in surprise and perhaps a little dismay. 'And I insist you take it. You've, as always, done an absolutely brilliant job with the fund-raiser. Enjoy your rest. You deserve it.' He smiled so charmingly that it didn't feel like a dismissal, although Emily was quite certain it was. He wasn't telling *her* to go take a taxi...and the thought filled her with fizzy bubbles again, the most delicious sort of anticipation.

Aimlessly, she wandered around the living room, waiting for Jason to return, her heart already starting a hectic beat. She saw a few half-drunk glasses of wine on a side table and reached for them, intending to take them to the kitchen.

'Leave that.'

Emily stilled, turned around. Jason stood in the doorway, his bow tie and the top button of his shirt undone, his hair just a little rumpled. He looked unbearably sexy. How had she ever thought he was boring? Now she felt so fizzy with anticipation and excitement she could barely breathe. 'Just trying to tidy up,' she said in a breathy, wobbly voice she barely recognised as her own.

'We can do it later.'

She swallowed down the question: *So what should we do now?* Her heart was beating so hard and fast it hurt and her palms were slick. She struggled to appear normal, as if *this* were normal, for her and Jason to be alone in his flat, the night dark all around them, his gaze steady on hers. She glanced around the stark black and white room with all of its after-party detritus. 'I think everyone had a lovely time, don't you?'

'I hope so.' He didn't sound very interested in continuing the conversation, and as he moved towards her Emily felt a lurch of something close to alarm. This was so new, so *strange*. This was *Jason*. And she still had a lurking fear that he was suddenly going to chuckle and say, *Oh, Emily, you didn't actually think...*

'I feel terrible about Philip and Helen,' she blurted, then wished she hadn't. They were just about the last two people on earth she wanted to talk about right now. It looked as if Jason felt the same for he stilled mid-stride, his brows drawing together.

'Do you?' he said neutrally, and Emily decided she might as well come clean. Better now than... later. If there was a later.

'Philip rang me last week,' she confessed. 'And it was obvious that he...that he didn't...' She stopped, wishing she'd never started this wretched conversation. 'I had no idea he was such a...a...'

'Bastard?' Jason supplied, and Emily nodded.

'Yes,' she admitted in a small voice. 'I'm afraid I really was blinded by his charm. And so was Helen.'

'Understandable, I suppose,' Jason replied. Emily watched as he removed his bow tie and slung it on a nearby chair. He certainly was very casual about removing his clothes. 'He's quite good at all that *sweeping*.' His gaze met hers, glinting with amusement, although she sensed something deeper, something darker underneath. Philip, Emily supposed, was a case in point for Jason. Sensible won over romantic. Except Philip really hadn't been either, in the end.

And Emily wasn't sure what Jason was being now.

'Yes…thank you for rescuing her from Philip this evening. I had no idea he would be here, or I wouldn't have invited her. I thought she could use a night out, away from Philip, and then of course he showed up with that Sylvie person, who builds *wells*, would you believe—'

'Emily,' Jason said, moving towards her, 'stop talking.'

Emily shut her mouth with a snap. She *had* been babbling, but she was so nervous. And Jason looked so assured. 'Okay,' she managed, her voice wobbling slightly. Jason stood in front of her, smiling faintly even as he drew his brows together in concern.

'Why are you so nervous?'

Emily shook her head, unwilling to admit how uncertain she still was. Even now she wasn't sure what Jason intended. What he wanted. She certainly knew what she wanted. Her gaze remained fixed on the column of his throat, the skin so smooth and warm-looking. 'I'm not nervous.'

'Really?' Jason arched an eyebrow, glancing pointedly at the pulse fluttering wildly in her throat. 'I wonder,' he said softly, his gaze now sweeping over her body like a blush, 'why the thought of me being anything other than boring, stuffy Jason terrifies you so much?'

Emily straightened her shoulders, her eyes flashing. 'Do I look terrified?'

'Do you really want to know the answer to that question?'

She let out an uncertain laugh, conceding the point. She supposed it did seem fairly obvious. 'Maybe not.'

'I think we've both needed to change the way we think about each other,' Jason continued, his voice musing, his gaze sweeping over her once more, lingering, languorous. Emily knew there could be no misinterpreting or imagining a look like that. His look was like a caress, his eyes touching her body. 'Of course, we might need some practical help in that regard.'

Only Jason would use the word *practical* in a moment like this. Emily didn't feel practical at all. Her entire body was buzzing with awareness, aching with need. 'Practical...?' she repeated in a whisper.

'Yes,' Jason confirmed, and he lifted a hand to tuck a stray tendril behind her ear, his fingers lingering on her lobe, that little touch possessive and sure. 'And the practical thing for me to do now is seduce you.'

CHAPTER NINE

'SEDUCE me?' Emily repeated. The words rippled over her, dousing her in shock. 'What is that supposed to mean?'

Jason laughed softly. 'I intend to show you in vivid detail.'

Images danced before Emily's eyes, intimate, evocative, startling images. Candlelight on bared skin, clothes slithering to the floor. 'What I meant was,' she amended hastily, 'that most people don't announce their intentions to *seduce*—'

'I told you I'd always be honest with you.'

'Ah.' She managed a shaky laugh. 'Right.' She was still reeling from Jason's sudden announcement. 'So seduction is practical, is it?' she said and Jason smiled.

'Eminently. You are attracted to me, aren't you?'

Emily flinched at such a direct question. There could be no evading, no protecting herself. Still, she tried. 'I… I suppose.'

He laughed softly. 'Damned with faint praise.'

Emily said nothing, not wanting to admit just how

attracted she was. Even now she was nervous, afraid. Terrified. Jason was right. The thought of him being anything other than what she'd known was scary, strange.

Thrilling.

'I suppose,' Jason murmured, 'I'll just have to convince you how attracted to me you are.'

Emily realised she'd just inadvertently issued another challenge with her tentative answer. She decided, despite the wild beating of her heart, to see it through. 'And how do you intend to do that?'

'Well…' He smiled and brushed another stray tendril of hair behind her ear. His fingers didn't even linger this time. Yet still it was enough for Emily to expel a breath in a ragged rush she couldn't quite control. 'Perhaps,' Jason murmured, 'I should start by kissing you.' Emily swallowed. Audibly. 'This time,' he told her, touching her chin with his fingertips, 'you won't ask me what it was for.'

Emily let out a shaky little laugh. 'Since you've already told me your intention, I won't have to.'

'Good.' And then he did kiss her, finally, and it was as unlike the last time as anything Emily could have imagined. There was nothing tentative about this kiss, nothing tenuous or tender or hesitant. This kiss was hot, hard, a searing brand that told Emily more than anything Jason had said or done just what he wanted to do. What he would do.

That she was his.

Her mouth opened under his, and she gasped

aloud as his tongue plunged inside, an erotic mimicry of what would surely come later. And even though Jason didn't move his hands or body or touch her in any other way, Emily was on fire. Liquid fire, her insides melting, her hands reaching up to grasp the lapels of his shirt, pressing closer to him, revelling in the feel of his body next to hers, hard against soft.

Jason broke the kiss with a smile; Emily felt his lips curve against hers. 'Oh, no, Emily,' he said softly. 'We're not rushing this.'

He called this rushing? Emily's face was flushed, her breathing already ragged, as if she'd just done a sprint. Or ten. Her hands were still fisted in his shirt. How could he look so unruffled? So in control?

But then Jason had always been in control. He was certainly calling the shots now. She was at his mercy, under his command.

'Fine,' she managed, shaking her hair over her shoulders. 'Take your time.'

Jason laughed softly. 'Oh, I will,' he assured her. 'I will.' He moved around her, his head cocked as if he were studying her. Underneath that steady, assessing gaze Emily felt suddenly vulnerable, conscious of the skimpiness of her form-fitting cocktail dress, the black silk hugging her rather generous curves. What was Jason thinking? Why was he looking at her so…thoroughly?

'You're beautiful,' he said. The words were spoken with such simple sincerity that Emily quivered. She'd been told she was beautiful before; her father said it all the time. She'd accepted it, taken it for granted even, yet she hadn't really *felt* it. Believed it. But she did when Jason told her in that honest, heartfelt tone. His voice echoed through her, filled her up to overflowing.

'Thank you,' she whispered, because she didn't know what else to say. 'You're not too bad yourself.'

Jason laughed softly. 'You're rather grudging with your compliments, aren't you?' He stood behind her now, and she felt his breath tickle the back of her neck. She tried not to shiver, but she could not suppress the urge, and when Jason pressed his lips to her nape she gasped aloud. She hadn't expected that, or for his hands to span her waist, sliding over the silk of her dress so he fitted her against him, and she leaned back, yielding to his touch.

She really did feel beautiful, sexy, *wanted*. She'd never felt so desired before, and it was the most intoxicating and powerful feeling in the world.

Slowly, savouring each bit of skin, he kissed his way from her neck to the sensitive curve of her shoulder, his hands sliding upwards from her hips. The sensation was achingly exquisite, almost too much, and they'd barely started.

'Jason—' she gasped, but stopped because she didn't know what to say. What to think. She could just feel this glorious spiralling inside of her, rising upwards, needing to be sated. Slowly, Jason slid his hands down to the hem of her dress, sliding it slowly, sensuously over her thighs. His fingers snagged on the tops of her stockings and he let out a choked laugh.

'God help me, you're wearing *garters*?'

Emily could barely think with his thumbs skimming the bare flesh of her thighs. 'They're…they're sensible,' she finally managed.

Jason slid his palm along the tender, exposed skin of her upper thigh, his thumb easily unhooking her garter. 'And I thought you didn't like sensible,' he murmured. 'Although if you call this sensible…' He moved around to her front and knelt before her. Emily watched, transfixed, as he slowly unrolled her stocking, his hands sliding along her knee and then calf and ankle until the stocking was crumpled on the floor and her leg was bare.

'Very sensible,' she said breathlessly as Jason started on the other leg. His head was bent and the light caught the gold glints of his hair amidst the brown. How had she ever thought his hair was boring? *He* was boring? He was the most exciting man she'd ever met. 'I don't like the feel of tights,' she explained, the words coming in fits and starts. She was mesmerised by the sight of him, by the feel of his hands on her skin. He'd unrolled the stocking and was now slowly peeling it away from her foot. 'Garters are more comfortable.'

'Comfortable and sensible,' Jason murmured. He tossed the stocking and garter to the ground. 'You sound as if you're speaking of orthopaedic shoes, not black lace garters.' He glanced up and Emily's breath dried in her throat at the look in his eyes. They blazed. She'd never seen Jason look so ferociously intense, so amazingly passionate…about her. The thought thrilled her, shook her to her core in a way that was both wonderful and a little frightening. She felt so *much*.

She was conscious then of her bare legs splayed out before her, her dress rucked up nearly to her waist. Slowly Jason slid his hands up her bare legs. Ankles, calves, knees. Emily had had no idea how erotic a touch to the leg could be. And when his hands came to her thighs and rested there possessively, fingers spread, as if he were taking ownership of her, she felt herself sway. Jason's hands, firm and sure, steadied her.

'Jason—' she said again, because she wanted his hands to slide upwards still. She wanted it desperately.

He smiled. He knew what she wanted. 'No rushing,' he reminded her, and then, still smiling, he slid his hands upwards and let his thumbs brush the silk of her underwear. Emily's knees buckled.

He was barely touching her, but it was enough. More than enough, and yet she still wanted more. Jason knelt before her, his hands still strong on her thighs and, leaning forward, he nipped at that scrap of lace with his teeth. Her hands fisted in his hair, half to draw him to her, half to push him away. She didn't know what she wanted. She wanted more, and yet part of her felt the intense vulnerability of having Jason before her like this, touching her in a way no one else ever had. Sex had never been like this before, but then this felt like so much more than sex.

They weren't even *having* sex yet, and already her mind and body were on physical and emotional overload. She didn't know if her body could take any more. If her heart could.

For surely her heart was involved. This wasn't just sex. This was a pure form of communication, elemental, essential. They were talking with their bodies, with hands and lips, and it was a language that was far more powerful than any words they might have spoken.

Jason must have sensed something of her struggle for he reached up and took her hands in his, wrapping his fingers around hers, and then placed them on his shoulders, anchoring her, so when he leaned forward again and pressed his mouth against her, she was actually using him to steady herself. To keep her balance and pull him even closer.

Emily's eyes closed, her body filled with a hot, restless yearning that was painful in its pleasure. It needed to end. She needed release.

Then she found it, and she cried out loud, a long jagged splinter of sound that ended as her body shook with sudden spasms of pleasure and her nails dug into Jason's shoulders.

Still holding her, he stood up, his body sliding

against hers. Emily sagged against him, weak with
the aftermath of spent desire. Jason easily scooped
her up in his arms, leading her to his bedroom and
that big black satin bed.

Emily let him carry her; she could hardly protest.
She felt as weak as a kitten, her body and mind both
utterly sated. Then Jason released her, her body sliding along his until she landed on her feet, and he
touched her chin with one finger.

'I said I was going to seduce you, but this is a
two-way street, Em.'

Her eyes fluttered open. 'Wh…what?'

'Do you think I'm going to do all the work?' He
arched an eyebrow, looking so much like the Jason
she knew that it was hard to reconcile him with
the man who had just touched her so intimately,
who had brought her a fierce pleasure she had never
known before.

'Work?' she said, thinking dazedly of Kingsley
Engineering and her position there. Jason, following her thoughts so easily, shook his head, smiling
slightly.

'Now it's your turn.'

He released her and Emily tried to get her bear-
ings. She felt as if she could barely stand, yet she
knew what Jason wanted. He wanted her to touch
him as he had touched her. They were equals in
this.

Emily gazed at him; he was still completely
dressed. So was she save her stockings, although

she felt as if she were nearly naked. She'd certainly shown more of herself than Jason had. She swallowed, wondering what to do. What Jason wanted her to do. She'd had two relationships before this, but sex had been a messy, fumbling affair in the dark. She hadn't known it could be anything else. She hadn't been that fussed, to be honest, because it had never occurred to her that it could actually be more. She wondered if that made her woefully naive, or just inexperienced. Both, she supposed.

'Em,' Jason prompted. There was laughter lurking in his voice, kind laughter that made Emily smile. 'Don't overanalyse this.'

'Really?' She gave him one of her old teasing smiles. 'I think you'd be the king of analysis. You probably have spreadsheets dedicated to the most effective technique.'

He laughed softly. 'Well, *spread* and *sheet* certainly figure into my thinking.' He reached for her hand, threading his fingers through hers, and guided it to his chest. 'Touch me.' There was a raw note of pleading in his voice, an unexpected vulnerability that spoke to Emily's heart and she realised just how much she wanted to touch him.

She laid her palm on his chest, spreading her fingers so his heart beat under her hand. She looked up and saw the longing in his eyes, and it nearly undid her. She'd had no idea how *emotional* this would be. The connection was as intimate as anything they were doing with their bodies, and just as new. Just as terrifying.

Slowly, she drew a breath and then laid her other hand on his chest. 'No rushing,' she reminded him, because now she was the one who needed to take her time.

'No rushing,' Jason assured her and, taking a deep breath, Emily started to undo the buttons of his shirt. Her fingers snagged on the studs of his tuxedo and she fumbled with the clasps, laughing a little bit as she realised unbuttoning his shirt was not going to be as easy as she'd hoped. So much for seeming experienced or sophisticated.

'Sorry,' she mumbled and Jason stilled her hands with his own.

'Next time I won't wear a tuxedo.'

Next time. The words sizzled through Emily's body, fried her mind. There was going to be a next time.

Quickly, Jason undid the studs and then shrugged out of his shirt and cumberbund, revealing the broad brown expanse of his chest. Emily laid her hands against the warm, taut skin, revelling in the feel of it. Of him.

She risked a glance upwards, saw Jason looking at her with almost a pained expression, a frown furrowing his forehead. She snatched her hands back. 'Wh…what? Am I—'

'I've just waited a long time for this.' He reached

for her hands, laughing softly. 'I'm starting to want to rush a little bit.'

The thought that her touch could inflame him so much was incredible. Incredibly powerful. Emily splayed her hands on his chest, let her fingernails scrape his skin. She heard Jason's rush of breath and smiled. 'Good things come to those who wait,' she told him softly, and Jason gave a laugh that sounded more like a shudder.

Emily let her hands drift down his chest, reached the waistband of his trousers. She felt powerful and a little shy. This was still Jason—*Jason*—and she could hardly believe any of this was happening. And might happen again.

'Emily…' Her name was a whisper, a hiss.

'Patience, remember?' Emily reminded him, her voice husky. Her heart had started to beat hard and fast again as she slid Jason's trousers down his legs. She'd felt so replete moments ago, but now desire was pooling deep inside her, causing that restless ache to surge through her body, demanding satiation.

Jason helped kick off his trousers, so all he wore was a pair of black silk boxers. Emily trailed her hands up the length of his legs, the crisp hairs tickling her palms. Taking another deep breath, she let her hand slide along the silk of his boxers, her fingers wrapping around the hard length hidden underneath before she continued to skim upwards, sliding along the hard, muscled wall of his chest, reaching for his shoulders.

Standing on her tiptoes, she kissed him. His mouth slackened under hers for an instant before he took control of the kiss, as she instinctively knew he would. She surrendered to it, to him, as his arms came around and he lifted her easily to the bed.

His hand tugged at the zip of the dress and he slid it off her easily, far more easily than she had managed with his own clothes. She lay on the bed, the satin duvet slippery under her, and felt a blush heat her body as Jason gazed at her. She wore only a skimpy black lace bra and thong, which had seemed sexy earlier but now felt indecent. She'd always liked sexy underwear, but nobody ever saw it except her. And now Jason.

'Incredible,' Jason whispered and bent his head to her breast. Emily stopped thinking. Sentences fragmented in her mind and died on her lips as sensation took over once more. Her fingers threaded in his hair as he continued his relentless onslaught, his lips moving over her skin as he undid her bra and slipped off her underwear. She felt him shrug out of his boxers and they were both finally naked.

The feel of his body against hers was another onslaught as every pressure point came into sharp and exquisite focus. Emily hooked her leg around his to draw him even closer, her arms wrapped around his shoulders, her mouth finding his again and again.

Now there was rushing, sweet wonderful rushing, as the need became too great to ignore, the desire too strong to resist.

'I've longed for this,' Jason whispered as he slid into her, and she felt her body open underneath him and accept him, and it amazed her in that instant how good it felt, how surprising and yet how right.

Nothing was strange about this moment. Nothing was embarrassing or awkward. It was all good.

It was wonderful.

And then she stopped thinking again, at least coherently. Thoughts blurred like colours and she felt her body arch in acceptance and deeper need as she pulled him closer still, matching him thrust for thrust, her face buried in the curve of his neck until the colours burst in a rainbow of sensation and they both fell back against the slippery pillows as if they were stars falling to earth, and the night exploded around them.

Neither of them spoke. Emily closed her eyes, her body replete, her heart full. From that fullness she acted, her arms coming around Jason, drawing her to him. Smiling, she kissed him, a soft, gentle kiss of both promise and gratitude.

She felt Jason tense, and then he kissed her back, gently, sweetly. Still smiling, Emily snuggled against him, fitting her body to his, and slept.

Jason felt Emily relax in his arms as her breathing evened out. She was asleep. Asleep in his bed, in his arms. He finally had what he wanted, and it was wonderful. Emily had been as sweetly generous with her body as she was in every other aspect of her life. Giving, honest and artless, and so very thrilling.

It couldn't last. He tensed again, as he had when she'd kissed him so sweetly, curling against him, utterly trusting and satisfied. He'd felt something in that kiss that he hadn't expected, wasn't sure he wanted. He couldn't want it.

This was just a fling, easy, enjoyable and with an end. Those were the terms. He'd convinced himself Emily understood that, wanted that, and yet now— with that kiss—a tendril of doubt unfurled inside him.

He really didn't want to hurt her. Yet he surely couldn't marry her. He needed a sensible wife, someone like him who valued the practical approach to marriage.

Not someone who wanted sweeping statements, grand gestures, a big romance—all things he didn't want, couldn't give. He wasn't that kind of man, never had been. He'd known it from childhood, seen it in his own father and knew he was of the same mould. He didn't want to disappoint his wife the way his father had his mother; he couldn't live with the devastating consequences.

He *wouldn't*.

A convenient marriage—agreed on both sides— was so much simpler.

Emily sighed in her sleep and Jason pushed the thoughts away. There was still time to find a suitable wife. Plenty of time. And right now he simply wanted to enjoy being with Emily. For however long it lasted.

CHAPTER TEN

EMILY woke slowly, blinking in the sunlight that slanted through Jason's floor-to-ceiling windows… the windows of his bedroom. She stretched, felt the slippery satin sheets slide against her naked limbs. A thrill ran through her, a thrill of excitement, re-membrance and just a little fear, as the memories from last night tumbled and arranged themselves in her mind.

Jason kissing her, touching her, inside her.

She turned, expecting to see him, but the bed was empty. A little splinter of disappointment needled her soul.

'Good morning.'

Emily turned to the sound of Jason's voice and saw him emerge from the en suite bathroom. He was showered and wearing a pair of faded jeans, his hair damp and his chest gloriously bare. He looked wonderful and also alarmingly energetic, while she was still lazing about in bed with her hair in rat's tails and last night's make-up caked and sticky on her face. She hiked the sheet up a little higher. 'Good morning.'

He smiled and tossed the towel he'd worn around his neck onto a bedpost. 'Coffee?'

Emily watched as he selected a shirt from a closet of frighteningly well-pressed clothes and slid it on. He sounded very brisk. 'Sure. I can make it.' She didn't move, though, because she didn't want to leave the bed naked and she didn't relish the idea of wearing last night's crumpled cocktail dress again.

'It's all right, it's already brewing.' Jason buttoned up his shirt, smiling at her, so clearly relaxed while she felt so horribly awkward.

Emily pushed a tendril of hair behind her ear, now stiff with old hairspray. 'Okay. I think I'll take a shower.'

'Great. You should fine everything you need in there.' *Except clothes.* He raked his fingers through his damp hair, so clearly relaxed, while Emily felt a little lost, a little lonely. A *lot* vulnerable. This was new territory, and she didn't know how to act or how to feel. She didn't feel strong or brave enough to manage her usual flippant tone. Giving her one last quick smile, Jason left the bedroom, whistling tunelessly as he went, and Emily slipped from the bed and hurried into the bathroom.

The hot, stinging spray of the shower felt good, healing, wiping away the traces of make-up and hairspray, everything except the ache in her heart.

Last night had been fun. A fling. She knew that.

She understood it, she'd accepted the terms. The rules. Jason had spelled them out clearly enough when he'd told her she wasn't in the running to be his wife. He'd reminded her again at Stephanie's wedding: *I want you, Emily. But I don't want you to be hurt.*

She'd harboured no illusions, no fantasies. This wasn't love; it wasn't even romantic. So why did she now feel such a yawning emptiness looming inside of her, as if she could tumble into its darkness and never return? Why did she feel so…*sad*?

She closed her eyes and let the water wash over her.

Love *always* had a habit of disappointing you.

Emily opened her eyes, the shampoo suds running into them and stinging. Why on earth had *that* word slipped into her mind? She didn't love Jason. She hadn't even considered such a thing. She didn't *want* to love him, didn't want to let herself in for even more disappointment.

Yet when she'd let him into her body, she'd cracked open the door to her heart. And now life had the potential—and Jason had the power—of not just disappointing her, but something far worse.

Hurt. Pain. Heartbreak.

That was why, despite the intense pleasure, last night felt like a mistake. A regret.

And she had no idea how to act—or feel—this morning. Jason obviously wasn't suffering from the same doubts. He'd been whistling, for heaven's sake.

He'd seemed energised and efficient and brisk. It terrified her; she didn't know how to respond to it. She didn't know anything.

Ten minutes later, her body near-scalded from the constant spray of hot water, Emily stepped out of the shower. She swathed herself in a towel and glanced hopelessly around Jason's bedroom for her discarded underwear. She did not feel like slipping into one of his shirts, acting cute and flirtatious. She felt dire.

She finally found the relevant garments, and did her best to smooth the wrinkles from her dress. She slipped it on, struggling with the zip in the back, and then brushed her hair and straightened her shoulders, ready—as she would ever be—to face Jason.

The sight of her discarded garters and stockings in the living room sent another pang of both pain and remembered pleasure through her, and she forced it aside as she stuffed her stockings in her bag and slipped her heels on her bare feet. Then she went to find Jason. She badly needed that cup of coffee.

Jason blinked in surprise as she came into the kitchen. 'You could have borrowed something of mine,' he said mildly, and handed her a mug of steaming coffee.

Emily wrapped her hands around the mug, grateful for its warmth. 'I'm fine,' she said, taking a sip. Her voice sounded stiff, brittle, and Jason noticed. He raised his eyebrows in silent enquiry, his gaze skimming over her. Emily knew she looked somewhat ridiculous. Her dress was crumpled, her legs bare, her hair wet. Worse, she felt suddenly near tears. There was no way she could tease or joke her way out of this, and from the look on Jason's face, he knew it.

'Emily,' he said. 'Come here.'

'What…?'

He put down his mug and held out his arms, and Emily blinked at him in shock for several seconds before her feet acted of their own accord and she went.

Jason's arms folded around her as he drew her snugly to him so her cheek rested on his shoulder and she breathed in the comforting smells of toothpaste and coffee, aftershave and the scent that was just Jason.

'I don't know how to be,' she confessed, snuffling a little against his shirt.

'Be yourself.'

She drew back to glance up at him, took in the kindness in his eyes, the hint of a smile around his mouth. 'But I'm not sure you even like it when I'm myself.'

'Like it?' Jason's brows snapped together in a sudden frown. 'What are you talking about, Em?'

She pushed a hank of wet hair behind her ear and tried to step out of his embrace. Jason's arms tightened around her; he wouldn't let her go. 'Be honest, Jason,' she said, although she wasn't sure she wanted him to be. 'You've always disapproved of me a little bit. You think I'm hopeless and scatty and who knows what else. I'm not—' She clamped down on that thought, her lips pressed tightly together. *I'm not even in the running.* Why was she thinking like this? Why did she care?

She should have sashayed out of Jason's bedroom wearing his shirt and her heels and tossed her hair over one shoulder, teasing him about how he wasn't *that* boring after all.

The words bubbled inside of her now but she knew they were too late because she'd already said too much. Revealed too much of how she really felt, what she was afraid of, and now she was left feeling exposed and vulnerable and *awful*.

This was why she avoided relationships, why she'd told Jason she wasn't interested in love. Love had the power to hurt you, because it never could live up to your expectations. You let someone see your weaknesses and fears and opened yourself up to all sorts of pain when they didn't feel the way you did, or they didn't act the way you wanted them to or they died…like her mother had, leaving her father to grieve these twenty years and more.

Thank God she didn't actually love Jason, she thought with a rush of relief. This was bad enough.

'I don't think you're hopeless,' Jason finally said, and Emily thought he sounded rather grudging.

'Scatty, then.'

'Emily—' He let out a little huff of breath, and

Emily could only imagine how all this talk of feelings was annoying him. This was not part of their understanding. 'Let me make you some breakfast,' he said instead, and Emily knew better than to press. She didn't really want to hear Jason tell her how he agreed with everything she'd just said and then top it off with a nonplussed *'so what?'*

'Fine,' she said, and then amended that ungracious reply with, 'Thank you. I usually just have toast in the mornings.'

'Which is why you're such a lightweight by dinner time,' he said, sliding her an amused glance. Emily conceded the point with a stiff smile. 'I'll make you eggs. It's the one thing I can actually make. You want the full fry-up?'

Emily didn't know how much she'd be able to choke down but at least if they were eating they wouldn't be talking. Saying things she didn't want to hear. 'Why not?' she said, tossing her hair, but it was wet and heavy and the gesture lacked the careless insouciance she'd been going for. Jason noticed, for he frowned slightly before turning towards the stove.

Jason concentrated on cracking eggs into a pan. He didn't want to have to see the uncertainty in Emily's clear green eyes. Of course the morning after was going to be strange; they had too much shared history for it to feel normal. Natural.

And yet holding her in his arms just then had felt

all too natural. Too right. He'd drawn her to him without thinking or analysing. He'd just acted. And it had felt good. He liked the way she fitted in his arms. He liked the way it made him feel.

The thought unsettled him. He didn't want to think about feelings, even if Emily seemed intent on pressing him to do so. He didn't want to think about the surprising rush of emotion he'd felt towards Emily last night, or even now.

This was just a fling. It had to be. Emily understood that; so did he. Yet right now, with the memory of last night still stirring through his body, all he knew was he didn't want to let her go.

'So do you cook for yourself when you're on these engineering projects of yours?' Emily asked. She'd hoisted herself up onto a bar stool, her dress riding up her thighs. Jason turned away, desire spiking through him once more, although he was relieved they were talking about more innocuous matters.

'Not really. When we're on site there is a catering team, but the food still is pretty basic. However, breakfast in most sub-Saharan countries is just a gruel made from cassava, and I've always been partial to a fried egg and toast.'

'So you learned to cook yourself breakfast there?'

'Actually, I learned to cook when I was younger,' Jason said. He kept his back to her, wanting to keep his voice light even though the question—and its answer—discomfited him. He wasn't sure he wanted to go into such personal territory. 'My mum died when I was eight, as you know, and my dad didn't cook at all.'

Emily was silent for a moment and Jason flipped the eggs over. He didn't particularly like to remember those lonely years, a house of taciturn silence and unspoken grief, painful memories. 'Almost everything I tried was a near disaster,' he continued lightly, 'but I did manage to make a decent fry-up.'

'That's more than I can say,' Emily replied, her voice as light as his. Still they somehow both managed to sound rather brittle. 'I can barely boil water.'

'What do you do, then?' Jason slid the fried eggs and toast onto two plates, giving her a knowing glance. 'Eat out?'

'Of course. I am *very* talented at speed-dialling.'

'A necessary skill in this day and age.' Jason passed the plate over to her. 'Dig in.'

'One of the few I have,' Emily agreed nonchalantly, and Jason had the feeling that she was trying to prove something to him. Was she actually trying to show him how scatty and hopeless she really was? He shook his head, unable—and perhaps unwilling—to understand the complicated working of the female mind. 'This is delicious,' she told him, her voice a bit more subdued. 'Thank you.'

* * *

The eggs were delicious, but Emily could barely swallow a mouthful. That moment in Jason's arms had both relieved and worried her, because it had felt too good to simply stand there, leaning against him, accepting his strength. Wanting more.

And even though she wanted to sit here and enjoy the breakfast and the time with Jason, the winter sunshine pouring through the huge windows, she couldn't. Her chest felt tight, her insides raw, and her brain was hammering home the realisation that she'd *known* this could have happened, that she'd been afraid of this all along.

She cared about him. And she couldn't allow herself to.

'So,' she said, dryly swallowing a mouthful of toast, 'how are you going to pick this paragon of yours?'

Jason looked up, his eyes narrowing. 'What are you talking about?'

Emily gave him a teasing smile. 'Your wife, Jason. You mentioned a list of candidates—'

'Actually, I didn't. You did.' He didn't look pleased by the turn in conversation.

'Only because I'm not one of them,' Emily reminded him sweetly. She smiled, even though it made her face hurt. Jason pressed his lips together in a hard line. Now he looked really annoyed, and she knew why. This was hardly morning-after conversation. She was picking a fight because it was better than bursting into tears, and she was perilously close to doing just that.

'I don't see the point to this conversation,' he said, a definite edge to his voice.

Emily arched her eyebrows. 'Does there need to be a point?'

'Emily—'

'I thought we were just making conversation. You *did* come back to London to find yourself a wife, didn't you? That's your personal business, isn't it?' Although he hadn't said as much, she could certainly put the pieces together. She might be scatty, but she wasn't stupid.

'In a manner of speaking,' Jason conceded after a moment.

'But since you're here with me, you must not be having any luck.'

'No, I'm not feeling lucky at all,' Jason snapped. 'Why are we talking about this, Emily? I think we both knew what we were getting into last night—'

'Of course. You seduced me. End of story.'

He let out an irritated breath. 'It was mutual, or so it seemed to me.'

She flashed him a quick cat-like smile. 'Absolutely.'

'Are you having regrets? Second thoughts?' he asked, the words coming out in staccato bullets, like gunfire.

Yes. And it was the last thing she'd admit to him now. She slipped off the stool. 'Of course not,' she said lightly. 'Why should I? I told you I never wanted to get married. And certainly not to you.' Emily knew how childish her words sounded, but she couldn't keep herself from saying them. Or the hurt from showing in her voice, her eyes. She hated feeling so vulnerable.

Jason's eyes narrowed to near slits, his mouth nothing more than a thin line. 'Then there's no problem,' he finally said, his voice so very neutral.

'None at all.' Except for the fact that she felt as if she might splinter apart in seconds. Still smiling, Emily turned and left the kitchen. Jason followed her out into the foyer, watched as she reached for her coat and jabbed her arms into the sleeves.

'Where are you going?'

'I have things to do,' Emily said, her back to him, her tone dismissive. 'I can't spend the whole day here, Jason.' She'd spend it huddled in bed with a box of tissues.

'All right,' Jason accepted after a moment. 'I'll see you at work on Monday.'

Emily didn't answer because she didn't know if she'd make it into work on Monday. She had a feeling she might call in sick.

Her back still to him, she jabbed the button for the lift. The silence ticked on between them, tautening with tension and unspoken words.

'Emily—' Jason said, just as the lift doors opened. She slipped quickly inside, turning only to waggle her fingers at him as they thankfully closed.

'Bye, then.'

The doors closed, but not before she saw Jason staring at her, a hard look on his face, his eyes narrowed as if he were trying to understand just what game she was playing.

Emily sagged against the wall as the lift sped downwards. Hopefully he would never know how much the last ten minutes had cost her.

Jason stood in the foyer, sifting through the last few minutes of conversation. He felt restless and annoyed and, bizarrely, a little hurt. That last emotion was ridiculous, because surely Emily was acting true to form, as he wanted her to. This was a fling, after all. She was…flinging.

So why didn't he like it?

Why did he feel as if he'd just been dismissed? Intentionally? *He* was the one who walked away, who left after one evening. One night. Yet Emily had just left him. The thought was aggravating. Insulting. *Hurtful.* He turned away from the lift doors, determined not to think of it, or why she'd gone so suddenly. Not to care. He had plenty of things he needed to do today, including drawing up that list of candidates Emily had mentioned. He did, after all, need to find a wife.

Even if the thought now filled him with a restless, aching discontent.

* * *

Emily lay in bed, staring at the ceiling. Her body and mind both ached and she wished she could find some kind of oblivion in sleep, but it eluded her. Her mind continued to run a looping reel of just about every moment she'd ever had with Jason, from that first tender dance to last night's soul-shattering events. Tears slipped down her cheeks in silent recrimination.

What was *wrong* with her?

She shouldn't be this sad, this *shattered*. Yet that was how she felt, as if all the secure pieces of her existence, her very self, had scattered and she was left with nothing, empty and aching inside.

Last night had changed the way she thought about life, about herself. The realisation scared her. She'd been *happy* before, content and confident, satisfied with her life. Then a single night with Jason Kingsley had made her feel as if all that—all of herself—had been flimsy and false. She'd been fooling herself all along, and it had taken last night—a night of incredible, intense intimacy, as well as this morning's hard wake-up call—to make her realise it.

She *wasn't* happy. She didn't know what she wanted…from Jason, or out of life itself. This was why she didn't do relationships, Emily thought miserably. They were either disappointing or devastating. Hugging her knees to her chest, she thought she'd take the disappointment she'd felt in her last two relationships over the swamping sense of loss she felt now. Then she'd been able to walk away with simple disillusionment rather than actual pain.

Now she felt as if she teetered on the precipice of a great, yawning chasm of heartache and it was only her refusal to probe too deeply into her own inner anguish that kept her from spiralling downwards into that endless space.

She didn't think. Wouldn't remember. Instead, she slipped down under the covers, pulling them over her head, and squeezed her eyes shut tight. She didn't know how long she lay there, willing sleep to come, but it finally did, and she existed in a deep, dreamless state where memories thankfully lost their power.

Of course, she couldn't sleep all day. She tried, but after a while her body's basic needs compelled her to rise from bed. She had a cup of tea and a piece of toast as she gazed moodily out of her window at a now snow-covered Hyde Park. It was going to be a white Christmas.

Christmas. She was meant to go home for Christmas on Wednesday, but Emily absolutely knew she could not go into work on Monday. She didn't even know if Jason would be there, but just the possibility was too awful to risk or even to contemplate. She'd been able to pretend—just—that she didn't care for a morning, but she couldn't do it for a whole day. Yet that was what her whole future looked like, day after day of pretending, until her heart stopped hurting and she forgot about Jason

Kingsley and the way he looked at her with those glinting eyes, the sound of his dry laughter, the feel of his mouth—

Except she couldn't forget about him because their families were related. He might even turn up in Surrey at Christmas. The thought of sitting down at the same table and passing the potatoes made her groan aloud.

How could she face any of it?

She'd ring work and say she was ill, Emily decided, and go home early. It was the coward's way out, but she felt like a coward. She was too cowardly even to face her own thoughts—or heart. She did not dare probe too much about how she felt about Jason, how deep the hurt ran. She was certainly not going to face him.

The thought of home with all of its dear familiarities, her father's welcoming arms and her sister's comforting presence, invigorated Emily and she grabbed a case from her cupboard and began to haphazardly throw clothes and cosmetics into it, desperate now to get away. To escape. Again.

Twenty miles from Highfield it had started to snow again, thick, fat flakes that drifted lazily down and completely obliterated the road in front of her. Emily tightened her grip on the steering wheel, her body tense—she'd been tense for hours, an entire day—as she willed herself and her vehicle onward.

When she finally turned into the sweeping

drive of Hartington House, its lights twinkling in the distance, the wheels of her car skidded on an icy crust of snow and impatiently she braked and turned off the engine, leaving the car half in a drift. She grabbed her case and headed up the drive, her feet soon soaked through. She didn't care. She just wanted to get home.

Her father met her at the door, wearing a shabby dressing gown and slippers. He looked shocked to see her, his eyes widening, a pipe forgotten in one hand.

'Emily! What on earth! I didn't think you were coming until Wednesday, darling.'

'I wasn't.' Emily stepped into the welcoming circle of her father's arms, breathed in the familiar scents of pipe tobacco and aftershave. 'I just wanted to come home,' she said, her voice muffled against his shoulder. She felt his hands stroke her hair and she closed her eyes, the unshed tears hot against her closed lids.

'Is everything all right, mouse?' he asked, using her nickname from her childhood. Emily sniffed and smiled.

'Yes,' she managed, and couldn't say any more.

Henry Wood squeezed her shoulders and stepped back. 'Well, it's good to have you. I'm afraid Carly has left for the night or I'd ask her to make up your bedroom.'

'It's all right.' Emily smiled, knowing her father would never have dreamed of making the bed himself. He was dear, but he was also stuck in his old-fashioned ways and he depended on his house-keeper. 'I'll do it myself.'

'We'll talk at breakfast,' Henry said and Emily nodded her acceptance.

It felt a little strange to be back in her childhood bedroom, although she'd spent just about every holi-day there since leaving Hartington House at the age of twenty. Yet now it felt different, because she felt different, and she wondered if life would ever be the same again.

Had she any idea what being with Jason would mean? Would cost her?

Refusing to think of it any more, she made up her bed and slipped gratefully under the sheets. Sleep, for once, came quickly.

The next morning the sun shone brightly over a world white with snow, and Emily felt her spirits lift just a little bit. Her father was already downstairs tucking into eggs and bacon when she joined him at the table.

They ate in silence for a little while; Henry had never been one to press for confidences. After a moment Emily cleared her throat and, looking at her father bent over his bacon, said, 'May I ask you something about Mum?'

Henry straightened, his expression one of surprise and, Emily thought, a little pain. Even twenty-two years after his wife's death, just the mention of her hurt. 'What do you want to know?'

He'd told her plenty of stories over the years, as had Isobel. Emily was the only one without any memories of her mother, beyond a vague, shadowy yet comforting presence. Yet the stories Henry and Isobel had told had been mostly about Elizabeth Wood as a mother. Now Emily wanted to know what she'd been like as a wife.

'You loved her very much…' she began hesitantly.

Henry's eyes widened. 'You have to ask?'

Emily shook her head, smiling a little bit. 'No. I know you did. You always told me how there wasn't another woman like her.'

'And there wasn't,' Henry said robustly. 'One in a million, your mother. One in a hundred million. She was perfect.' He shook his head, his expression fading into a sorrowful reflectiveness. 'I was a lucky sod, you know, that she loved me back. An old grump like me. She was everything to me, Emily, everything.'

Emily swallowed, her throat tight. 'You still miss her.'

'Every day,' Henry said simply. 'I'll never stop. But it's easier now than it was. Those first few years… Well, you don't remember, but they were dark days.' He shook his head. 'I wasn't sure I could go on living without her. She was my anchor, my very soul. But I had you and Izzy to look after, and thank God I did, because I couldn't ever imagine life without you.'

'And,' Emily asked, the words no more than a whisper, 'do you ever—do you ever regret loving her so much? Since you lost her?'

Henry looked at her shrewdly for a moment before answering. 'Not for one second. Not one bit.' He smiled a bit sadly, and Emily suddenly saw how white his hair was, how lined his face. Her father had married late in life and he was already well into his seventies. He looked his age, the years of grief etched on his dear face. Her throat tightened with emotion. 'Loving your mother was the best thing I ever did, Emily. Don't ever doubt it.'

Emily nodded, accepting. The risk had been worth it for her father, she knew that. The love he'd had with her mother had been rare, overwhelming, precious. And nothing like what was—or had been—between her and Jason.

Yet that, she knew now, was what she wanted. Love. Romance. To be swept off her feet.

If you're swept off your feet...you might even fall.

Recalling Jason's words, she acknowledged how true they unfortunately were. She'd fallen. Hard.

Emily spent the days before Christmas tucked away at Hartington House, grateful to avoid the rush of the holiday season. She visited her sister and Jack at their home in a neighbouring village, a relaxed sprawl of a place where children and dogs ran amok amid the cheerful chaos of family life. She watched their easy banter and their casual affection with envy, a jealousy she had never felt before but had now sunk its razor claws into her soul.

She wanted that. All of it. And she'd never realised how much until she'd experienced a tiny taste of it with Jason. Of course, she knew how appalled he'd be if she were ever to tell him. *That* was not part of his precious agenda. She was the fling, not the wife. The bit of fun before he settled down, she supposed, and she could hardly blame him. She'd presented herself as just that, blithely informing him that love and marriage were well and good for other people, but not for her. She wanted to have *fun*.

Well, she'd had her fun. And in the end it hadn't been very fun at all.

Would he announce his engagement to whatever practical paragon he chose at Christmas? Easter? Would she have to attend the wedding, smile for the photographs? It was all just too awful to think about, yet Emily spent endless hours torturing herself by doing just that.

On Christmas Eve she was finally forced out of her moody lethargy. 'I haven't even asked what we're doing for Christmas dinner tomorrow,' Emily said as she sat down to breakfast with her father. She'd bought presents, at least, but she wasn't feeling very festive.

'Oh, don't worry, it's all taken care of,' Henry assured her with a wave of his hand.

'Isobel's arranging something, I suppose?' Her sister had always been the organised one.

'No, no, Izzy's taking some time off this year,' Henry said. 'Actually, we've all been invited over to Weldon. Jason's coming home.'

CHAPTER ELEVEN

EMILY slid out of her father's car and gazed up at the ancient, imposing Weldon Manor with trepidation and foreboding. Jason was in that house. Just the thought of seeing him again sent her nerves jangling, her palms sweating and her heart beating far too hard.

'Ready, darling?' Henry smiled at her, and Emily was assailed again with how old he looked. He wasn't quite frail, but he picked his way over the uneven cobblestones of the Manor drive with care. Emily slid her arm through his, steadying him without seeming to.

'This should be fun,' she said, attempting airiness. 'A nice family gathering.' *If only.*

Henry gestured to the Land Rover already parked in the drive. 'Looks like Izzy and Jack have already arrived.'

Fortunately Isobel was the one who opened the door and even as Emily glanced furtively around the huge, soaring entrance hall Jason was nowhere in sight. She let herself be enveloped in hugs and tackled around the knees by her niece and nephew, grateful for the temporary reprieve.

Of course it couldn't last for ever. This was Jason's home, after all. His father's home. Edward Kingsley welcomed them into the front drawing room for sherry by the fire, presiding over the gathering like a king on his throne, polite yet distant, a little bit remote. A little bit like Jason. Neither man, it seemed, was given to much emotion.

Emily accepted her glass of sherry and stood by the window, half-hidden by the curtains. She looked away when Jason strolled into the room, his manner relaxed and assured. Unlike her.

'Jason!' All smiles, Isobel crossed the room to embrace her brother-in-law. 'We haven't seen you in an age. It's so good to have you back.'

'It's good to be back,' Jason replied, kissing her cheek. Emily felt his gaze move over her like a shadow even though she was pretending a deep and abiding interest in the view of the snowy front lawn outside.

She couldn't focus on her sister's cheerful chatter; every muscle and nerve was concentrated on maintaining this attitude of relaxed disinterest. She had a feeling she was failing miserably.

'And you must see if you can cheer Emily out of her blues,' Isobel continued playfully. Emily stiffened at the mention of her name.

'The blues?' Jason repeated neutrally.

'Yes, she hasn't been herself, have you, darling?'

Isobel smiled at Emily, who tried to give her a quelling look without Jason noticing. It proved impossible, or her sister simply ignored it. Isobel pursed her lips knowingly. 'Is it a man, Emily?'

She felt herself flush and her fingers clenched so tightly around her sherry glass she thought she might snap its fragile stem. 'No, of course not,' she said, her voice sounding stiff and awkward. 'Why would you think that?'

'Because you've been positively moping. And it's *Christmas.*'

'Isobel—' Emily spoke warningly, not that her sister ever heeded such warnings. She was bossy in the most lovable way, yet right now Emily felt like strangling her.

'Well,' Jason said, and Emily's gaze instinctively flew to him, drinking him in despite her intentions to appear unmoved. His cheeks were still flushed with cold, his eyes bright and glinting. 'We'll have to see what we can do about that.' His gaze rested on her, so knowing, so assured, and, panicking, Emily wondered what he could possibly mean by that statement.

'I'm fine,' she said rather sharply, looking away again. 'You don't need to do anything.'

Edward Kingsley cleared his throat, surely a sign that this discussion was over. Undoubtedly it had become too personal for his taste.

* * *

Jason watched Emily walk stiffly from the room, her head held high, her body radiating tension. She'd been jumpy as a cat since he'd arrived. He'd had a lot of time to think about what had happened the morning after their night together, to consider why Emily had left so suddenly—and why he had been so aggravated by her departure.

He wasn't used to such reflection, and he didn't particularly enjoy it. He was a man of action, not thoughts. Not words. Words, he well knew, accomplished little. Meant nothing. Made no difference.

He wanted to act, to accomplish and to complete. And after almost a week of thinking about Emily, about that alleged list of wifely candidates, he'd had enough. He knew what he wanted. And he knew what he was going to do.

It was just a matter of presenting his plan to Emily.

Even with Isobel's steady chatter, Christmas dinner felt stilted. Of course, Jason was used to these heavy silences; they had defined his youth, ever since his mother's death. His father was a man of few feelings or words, and he'd moulded his oldest son to his likeness. Jack had been the rebel, not Jason.

Yet now he felt more than ever the oppressiveness of his father's presence, his silence, the grim dourness of Weldon Manor—all the more apparent when Emily sat across from him, as beautiful and brilliant as a butterfly.

He pictured her moving among the dark, heavy rooms of the house, filling them with light and laughter. If she was willing to let go of some of her childish flights of fancy—and he thought she might be—they could have a good life together. He hoped she would, for once, see sense.

He waited until after dinner, when everyone had retired back to the drawing room. Isobel was putting the baby down for a nap and Jack was deep in conversation with his father-in-law; Edward Kingsley had retreated to his study.

Jason turned to Emily. 'Why don't we go for a walk? It's beautiful outside.'

She looked startled, and trapped, and even afraid. 'I…'

'I think that's a wonderful idea,' Isobel said, coming back into the drawing room, now child-free. 'You can get some fresh air. And I'm sure you'll cheer her up, won't you, Jason?'

'I intend to.'

Emily looked as if she still wanted to resist but, with a shrug she capitulated. 'I'll just get my coat.'

Jason waited for her by the back door, smiling easily as she joined him with obvious reluctance and they headed out into the Manor's landscaped gardens, now blanketed in snow.

It was a beautiful, brilliant day, the sky a hard, bright blue and the air clean and sharp. The trees that lined the stone walk through the garden were encased in ice, every twig and branch glittering with sunlight.

'Why didn't you come to work on Monday?' Jason asked after a few minutes of walking and Emily stiffened.

'I'm sorry if it inconvenienced you,' she said stiltedly, 'but I am entitled to several personal days—'

'Emily, I'm not asking as your boss,' Jason cut her off, keeping his voice mild. 'I'm asking as your lover.'

She stared at him, her eyes wide, her mouth slightly parted. Clearly shocked. 'I needed some time,' she said after a moment, her voice low. 'To think.'

He'd thought, too. He wondered if they'd come to the same conclusions. If they hadn't, he thought he could convince her with certain…methods. 'And did you?' he enquired. 'Think?'

'Yes.' She didn't say anything more and they kept walking, the only sound the crunch of their boots in the snow. 'I don't think this is going to work,' Emily finally said. Her voice was barely audible, her eyes on the ground. 'Whatever it is. A fling. An affair.'

'Oh?' He kept his voice neutral, waiting to hear what she said. What she thought.

'No. I've…I've realised I want something different.'

'And what is it that you want?'

'It doesn't matter,' she said quickly. 'The night we had together was pleasurable, Jason, you know that, but—' She stopped, turning to look at him with heartbreaking honesty. 'I think it's better if we just stay…friends.'

'That is an idea,' Jason allowed, stopping, as well. He gazed at her, taking in her tousled hair, her wide jade eyes, the lush fullness of her parted lips. He wanted to pull her into his arms, to kiss her until they were both breathless, but he waited. First there were things he needed to say. 'I have another idea.'

Her eyes widened, her face so open and artless. She hid nothing. 'You do?'

'Yes. I want you to marry me.'

Jason's words echoed in Emily's brain, but they didn't make sense. Surely he hadn't said—hadn't suggested—

'What did you say?' she managed, her voice no more than a thready whisper.

'I want you to marry me, Emily. I've been thinking about it all week and I've realised it makes sense.'

'Makes sense,' Emily repeated numbly. He sounded so *reasonable*.

'I told you I was looking for a wife—'

'And you also told me I wasn't in the running,' she reminded him. She heard the hurt in her voice and didn't care. She was feeling too overwhelmed, too incredulous, too *furious* to hide her emotions now.

Jason looked a tiny bit discomfited, but then he

smiled easily and spread his hands wide. 'I changed my mind.'

'Oh, you did, did you?' She let out a laugh, abrupt and sharp, like a gunshot. 'So was that a proposal?'

Again she saw that annoyance flash across his features. She supposed this wasn't the conversation he'd intended on having.

'Call it what you will. We're good together, Emily. You can't deny that—'

'In bed, maybe.'

'Out of it, as well,' Jason said firmly. 'I'm not suggesting a marriage based purely on physical attraction.'

'Oh, no, I'm sure you have several other practical considerations,' Emily retorted. She was angry, perhaps unreasonably so, but it was better than bawling, which was what she felt like doing, because she hadn't, in a million years, expected this. Or how much it would hurt.

And she'd thought *making a go of it* was bad. This was infinitely worse.

'As a matter of fact, yes,' Jason said calmly. He was obviously on familiar territory now. Emily folded her arms and waited. 'We come from a similar background, our families are friendly, we're compatible physically and, I believe, emotionally.'

'Emotionally?' Emily repeated in disbelief. It wasn't a word she'd expected him to use. And as far as *compatibility* went—

'Yes. We complement each other, Em. We're different, I know that, but that can be a good thing.'

She didn't bother asking how. She wasn't sure she wanted to know. *I'll keep you from being completely irresponsible...* 'That's quite a list you've got.'

'And, most importantly,' Jason continued, as if delivering the coup de grâce, 'we're realistic about love.'

She swallowed. Her heart felt like a stone. 'We are?'

'You said so yourself,' Jason reminded her. 'You told me you weren't waiting for Prince Charming to rescue you. You agreed it was overrated. You're happy as you are.' He parroted back all the statements she'd given him with such breezy—and false—confidence. Obviously she'd been too convincing; he'd actually believed her.

'If I'm so happy, why should I get married?'

'Children, companionship, sex.' Yet another list. How could he be so sensible—so heartless—about the rest of their lives? About each other?

'So,' Emily managed through stiff lips, 'why did you change your mind? How did I suddenly become so suitable?' Jason hesitated, and for the first time he seemed truly at a loss for words. Emily shook her head. She didn't really want to hear how he'd made some kind of pro and con list. *Pros: sex. Cons: hopelessly scatty.* 'It doesn't matter. I'm not going to marry you, Jason.'

His brows snapped together. 'And do you have a reason?'

She almost laughed. Yes, she did, a great, big, obvious and awful one. 'You don't love me.' It hurt to say the words, to feel them, because she knew in that moment that she loved Jason. It had been building inside her, the pressure mounting, the knowledge inarguable and consuming. She'd done exactly what she hadn't wanted to do, and fallen in love. And she'd done it with someone who had no interest in love even as a concept. She'd found that rare, precious thing called love; unfortunately it hadn't found her.

How had she fooled herself even for a moment that she didn't love him? Of course she did. That was why she'd been so nervous about being involved with Jason in the first place, why she'd never been able to forget that dance. That kiss. Why she'd run away the morning after they'd made…had sex. Because that was all it had been. Sex. And she'd been running and hiding from the truth of her feelings, her desires, because she hadn't wanted to face this moment, when he looked at her with a blank confusion that stated so clearly the idea of loving her hadn't even crossed his mind.

Jason was silent for a long moment. 'Anyone can tell you he loves you,' he finally said.

Except you, Emily thought miserably. She blinked hard. 'Well, obviously he needs to mean it.' She dragged in a desperate breath. 'And, in any case, it's not just about words. It's about feelings and… and actions.'

Jason gazed at her levelly. 'And what actions have made you think I don't love you?'

She blinked again, trying to focus. Was he trying to trick her with that question? He was trapping her somehow, Emily could see it in his narrowed gaze, the dangerous glitter in those honeyed eyes. She struggled to frame an honest response. 'Because this conversation would have gone very differently if you did,' she finally said.

'Would it?' Jason challenged. 'You came into this conversation with some kind of preconceived notion about what love is, didn't you? You'd already decided whatever I felt—whatever I did—wasn't enough. Because you want something more.' Each word was delivered like a hammer blow, an attack on everything she felt. 'And maybe you don't even know what that is, but it's always got to be more. You want me to tell you I can't live without you, that life would be hell if you're not in it. You want roses and rings and maybe even tears. Don't you?' His voice rang out, strong and scornful, and yet underneath Emily detected a thread of hurt. And she knew that she couldn't blame Jason for not loving her; they'd both come to this sorry point. They simply wanted different things. She was asking for something he was incapable of giving.

She tried to smile and failed. Her lips moved at least. 'Maybe not the tears,' she conceded. 'A sniffle would do. But yes, I do want those things. I want the fairy tale.'

'And that's just what it is. A fairy tale.' He dug his hands into the pockets of his coat, shaking his head as he turned away from her. 'That's why I don't want a marriage based on love. It's fickle, fleeting, and it makes you unhappy. I thought you'd see sense—'

She tried to laugh, but it sounded more like a bark. 'When have I ever seen sense?'

The anger seemed to seep out of Jason, leaving him silent, even defeated. He turned to her with a small, sad smile. 'I suppose I'm the one who hasn't been sensible, convincing myself that you wanted the same thing I did, that you didn't care about love and romance and the rest.' He looked at her ruefully, trying to lighten the moment, although his eyes were still shadowed. 'If I'd really thought about it I'd know it was utter bunk. You've been pairing everyone else into happily-ever-afters. Of course you want the same for yourself.'

She sniffed. Loudly. 'Yes, I do.'

'And my idea for a happily-ever-after isn't the same as yours.' He paused, his voice quiet. 'It isn't enough.'

Emily's heart twisted. Tore. She felt as if she'd failed him somehow, as if she were being demanding and unreasonable by wanting that most elemental and ephemeral thing, *love*. And part of her wanted to tell him that it didn't matter, that maybe her love could be enough for both of them. But she knew it couldn't.

'It's better this way, I suppose, than to realise later.' He paused, his gaze turning distant. 'I've seen how different expectations from a marriage can make things miserable. A living hell, in fact.' He gave a short, rather cold laugh, and Emily stiffened, surprised by this sudden intimacy, this peek into Jason's personal life that she'd never even known about. 'My parents had that. My father has never been a very expressive man, and I don't know if he loved my mother. I know he never told her.' He paused, his throat working, and Emily knew how hard this must be for him to say. 'She certainly didn't know. She became more and more unhappy, wanting something from him that he could never give.' He glanced at her, his lips twisting in a rather grim smile. 'Words. Gestures. All these proofs of love that are meaningless—'

Plastic-wrapped bouquets and meaningless compliments. 'But they're not meaningless if you really do mean them, Jason,' Emily said quietly. 'If there's something behind the words. The gestures.' She paused, then dredged up the courage to say quietly, 'If you love me.'

He stared at her, his face like a mask, a curtain coming down over his eyes, his heart. She couldn't see in. She didn't know what he was thinking, but he certainly didn't need to say any words to confirm the awful truth: he didn't love her. Why was she torturing herself this way? 'Tell me,' she asked, her throat raw and scratchy, the tears crowding the corners of her eyes and then sliding down her face, 'have you ever told anyone you loved them?' She swiped at her wet cheeks, her tears already freezing in the winter air.

Jason did not answer for an endless, aching moment. Finally, he said in a voice Emily could barely hear, 'Once.'

He didn't elaborate and Emily stared at him sadly. 'And what happened?'

'It was my mother,' he said, the words drawn from him with deep and obvious reluctance. 'And she didn't say anything.' He pressed his lips together, clearly finished.

There had to be more to that memory than Jason seemed willing to tell, Emily thought. Perhaps it held a clue or even a key to why he was so reluctant to love anyone now. She sighed, the sound trembling with suppressed emotion. 'We're a sorry pair.'

'Aren't we just.'

They both lapsed into a silence of sorrow, an ocean of regret opening up between them. Jason let out a ragged sigh and nodded towards the Manor, looming in the distance, a darkened hulk against the violet sky. Twilight had crept over the countryside without her even realising it; darkness had come. 'You should go in. You look cold.'

'Aren't…aren't you coming?'

Jason shook his head, his gaze on the distance, his expression remote. 'I'll walk a bit longer.'

And silently, because there was really nothing more to say, Emily turned and went back inside the house.

When Jason returned an hour later, he barely looked at her. He brushed off Isobel's fussing that he must have frozen himself to death, and accepted Jack's good-natured teasing that he preferred the cold to being inside with the lot of them. When Emily sneaked glances at him, his expression was sometimes blank, sometimes brooding, and gave her no insight as to how he really felt.

Yet it shouldn't even matter, because everything had already been said. The only option now was to pick up the pieces of her broken heart and cobble them together, carrying on, just like before. Perhaps Jason's personal business would conclude sooner than he anticipated and he'd return to Africa or Asia or wherever his next engineering project would take him.

Yet even that thought gave her a weary pang. She'd miss him. She missed him already.

The hour slogging through the snow had numbed Jason's heart and mind, as well as his body. He needed that numbness because the conversation with Emily had opened up too many feelings, too many regrets. Too many memories.

Have you ever told anyone you loved them?

Once.

For a moment, in his mind's eye, Jason could see his mother's pale face, the tears sliding silently down her waxen cheeks. He heard his stammering protest that *he* loved her at least, and watched her turn her face to the wall.

It was the last time he'd ever seen her alive.

He pushed the memory down, not wanting to deal with the swamping sense of devastation and loneliness it caused. There was a reason he never thought of it. A reason he'd decided to pursue a marriage of convenience, a marriage without the pain and disappointment of love.

Love hurt. It hurt the person loved and the person loving. It was messy, disappointing, complicated and unnecessary. He'd witnessed his parents' marriage crumble to nothing, seen his mother collapse into herself because his father could never give her what she wanted. As an adult he'd realised his mother had most likely been suffering from depression, which had contributed to her unhappiness in her marriage. He knew plenty of people fell in love, believed the fairy tale. Lived it. Yet he wasn't willing to take the risk. He was too like his father, sensible, silent, unwilling to say those three little words.

Have you ever told anyone you loved them?
Once.

And that was why—at least in part—he never planned to say—or feel—it again.

CHAPTER TWELVE

THE snow had turned to slush by the time Emily returned to work after New Year's. Her mood matched the dreary weather, as it had since that last painful conversation with Jason. She hadn't seen him since Christmas Day; he'd left Weldon that afternoon to drive back to London and work.

Now, as she dragged herself back to the office, she wondered if she'd see him. What he would say. What *she* would say. Her mind felt empty of words or even thoughts. She felt numb, although it was the kind of numbness that still allowed her to be aware of the yawning unhappiness fogging the fringes of her mind; she felt as if she were skating on very thin ice and at any time she could crash through and drown in the churning emotions below.

Helen greeted her at reception, looking bright-eyed and rosy-cheeked. She seemed, Emily thought with equal parts relief and resentment, to have recovered from Philip's put-down.

'Happy Christmas, Emily!' Helen called out. 'Or

should I say Happy New Years? In any case, it's glorious out, isn't it?'

Emily glanced over her shoulder at the icy, needling drizzle and made a face. 'I don't know if glorious is the term I'd choose.'

Helen blushed, making her look lovelier than ever. 'Oh, no, I suppose…it's just…I'm so *happy*.'

'That's certainly good to hear.' Helen's obvious cheer lifted Emily's own sagging spirits a little. 'You had a nice holiday?'

'Oh, yes.' Helen leaned forward. 'I know you're going to think me so scatty, but I'm not broken up over—' she nibbled her lip '—you-know-who any more.'

'I'm glad to hear that.' Even if she still felt guilty. And miserable. 'I'm so sorr—'

'No, no, don't be sorry,' Helen said quickly. 'Really, it's fine. And—' she glanced up shyly at Emily, her face colouring a little more '—there's someone else now.'

'There is?' Emily tried to keep the note of surprise—and perhaps even censure—from her voice. 'Well, that's…that's wonderful. And I suppose by how happy you are he feels the same?'

'I think he does,' Helen said, and Emily wondered if a word of caution might be needed. Clearly there had been some misunderstanding in the past. If Helen needed advice, however, she was hardly the person to give it. 'I know he does,' Helen stated firmly, and Emily decided not to press.

'Well, who is this lucky man?'

'I don't know if you'll approve—'

'Oh, Helen, you hardly need my approval.' Emily smiled, suppressing a weary sigh. 'I've obviously proved myself to be quite useless at matchmaking, and at relationships in general, for that matter. I'm sure the two of you will be fine.'

'It's Richard,' Helen admitted in a whisper, and Emily stared at her in surprise.

'But—'

'He asked me to marry him,' Helen confessed in a rush. 'I didn't say yes yet, but he really is so kind and I know he'll treat me right—'

Emily swallowed down the words she wanted to say. She would not offer advice. Not any more. 'And do you think that will be enough?'

'What more is there?' Helen asked simply and Emily let out a little laugh.

'Not much, I suppose.' Roses and proclamations of love and being swept off your feet. Romance. Passion. Love.

Plastic-wrapped bouquets and meaningless compliments.

Jason would quite approve of Helen's statement, Emily thought as she headed up to her office. She felt like the last person in the world who still believed in love. In something more.

Back in her office, Emily sank into her seat, her fingers rubbing her temples. She felt the beginnings of a headache coming on, but it was nothing compared to the misery swamping her soul. When did it get better? How?

She wondered if she should change jobs, just to give herself a little space from Jason. Even if he spent every second in Africa, or wherever else, this was still his company and there were reminders of him everywhere. Yet the thought of leaving Kingsley Engineering—and any chance to be near Jason, however small—was heart-wrenching.

She really was a mess, Emily thought as she switched on her computer. After years of feeling breezily confident and put together, of arranging other people's lives and being so very sure of her own, she was now coming apart at the seams. Had it all been a mirage, a *lie* all this time, and this was who she really was—and how she really felt?

Grimly, Emily had to acknowledge that this overwhelming love for Jason had not sprung suddenly over the course of a single night. It had been there all along, quietly growing, from the moment he'd taken her into his arms at her sister's wedding—or perhaps before then. Who even knew how long she'd loved Jason? He'd been so much a part of her life, and yet now he was the most important part, and he wasn't even in it any more.

Emily pushed the thoughts away, knowing these painful reflections would only become maudlin if she continued to indulge herself in useless recriminations. Reaching for her coffee mug, she straightened her shoulders and prepared for a long day of work.

The days passed slowly, marked by their mundanity. And the absence of Jason. Once again he remained out of the office, and Emily couldn't bring herself to ask his assistant or anyone else where he might be. It was, so very clearly, none of her business.

So when Jason's PA telephoned her a week later, she received the urgent summons to his office with surprise, trepidation and even a little terror.

'You mean…now?'

'Yes, Mr Kingsley's waiting.'

'I'll be right there.' Emily hung up the phone, trying to quiet the swarm of butterflies that had just taken residence in her stomach and now threatened to crawl up her throat. She'd never been so urgently summoned to Jason's office. She hadn't even been in his office in years.

What did he want?

Already her mind—and heart—leapt ahead, imagining a most unlikely scenario. He'd changed his mind. He realised he loved her.

Forget what I said before, Em. I was crazy to think I could last a day without you…

Somehow Emily knew that was not what Jason intended to say. Anyway, he'd already lasted well over a week. After checking her reflection in the mirror—she looked pale, but composed—she headed upstairs to the CEO's office.

Eloise, his PA, nodded briskly as Emily stepped into the reception area in front of a pair of closed mahogany doors.

'Go right in, Emily. He's waiting.'

Good heavens, was she in trouble? Was she going to be *fired*? Was this Jason's way of excising her from his life? He didn't need to leave; she would.

Swallowing down her nerves, Emily turned the handle of one of the doors and slipped into Jason's huge, sumptuous office.

He stood at the far end, behind his desk, his back to her as he surveyed the panoramic view of the city. Emily took a few hesitant steps inside. Her heart beat wildly and she didn't trust herself to speak, or at least to sound normal.

After a long, torturous moment Jason turned around. His dark eyes swept over her and there was no glint of amusement, no welcoming smile. No dimple. His expression looked frighteningly sober. 'Hello, Emily.'

Emily nodded her own greeting. She still didn't think she could speak. A huge lump had risen in her throat and it was making everything inside her ache.

Jason surveyed her quietly, his gaze seeming not just to take her in but to *memorise* her, and Emily suddenly had an awful feeling about why she'd been summoned to his office. The last faint flicker of hope that he'd changed his mind crumbled to ash. Stupid of her to have even entertained such an idea for a second. The only reason Jason would look at her like that was because he was going to say goodbye.

'You wanted to speak to me?' she finally managed to ask in a husky whisper.

'I wanted to say goodbye,' Jason said. 'I'm leaving. To Brazil this time. There's a dam being built on the Parana River and they've asked me to come in as a consultant.'

'Oh.' Emily cleared her throat, trying to ignore the searing pain of loss this announcement caused her. It shouldn't matter, yet it did. It hurt, unbearably. 'I thought you were staying in London for a while.'

'Well—' Jason smiled crookedly '—I've concluded my personal business for the moment.'

'You mean finding a wife,' she said flatly. *Business.* He shrugged his assent and Emily forced the words out. 'So who did you decide on, in the end?'

He stared at her, unspeaking, as if he were trying to make sense of her words. 'You think I found someone else to marry in the last ten days?' He shook his head in disbelief. 'I may be a bit sensible for your liking, Emily, but I'm not completely heartless. No, I've decided not to pursue marriage at this time.'

He sounded as if he were talking about a corporate merger. *At this time.* Well, he would eventually. He'd find someone who agreed with his plan, who liked his lists. It just wasn't—couldn't be—her. Even if at this moment she wanted it to be.

'Well,' she said when she trusted her voice, 'I don't think there's any pressing business in HR you need to—'

'*Emily*—' Jason's voice sounded a raw note of pain she hadn't expected '—do you think I called you up here to talk about HR?'

'Considering the kind of summons I received, I assumed it was *business*,' Emily replied stiffly.

Jason rubbed a hand over his face. He suddenly looked incredibly weary. 'I'm sorry if that's the way it seemed. I simply wanted to say goodbye. My plane leaves this afternoon.'

'Oh.' Emily swallowed. 'Well…' She tried to smile. She did, but instead she found the corners of her mouth turning down. 'Have a good—' She couldn't finish the sentence because her voice wobbled all too revealingly. Before she could even feel the wash of humiliation this caused, Jason strode towards her and in one swift, sure movement he took her by the shoulders and pulled her towards him.

Shock and then pleasure raced through her as his lips came down hard on hers and he kissed her with all the pent-up sorrow and ferocity she'd thought only she felt. And, as her body kicked into its overwhelming physical response, her breasts colliding with his chest, her fingers threading through his hair, her mind insisted on dismissing whatever didn't work between them. She wanted love? Forget it. She needed romance? It didn't matter. She could live without them as long as they had *this*...

Yet, even as her body was clamouring for him and her mind was insisting it was enough, her heart knew better. And when Jason released her so abruptly that she took a stumbling step backwards, she didn't speak. Jason did.

'Goodbye,' he said and turned away from her.

Emily stood there for a moment, bereft, humiliated, *aching* as the tears crowded her eyes and stung her lids. She blinked hard, swallowed down the restless churn of emotions Jason's kiss had caused and left his office without another word.

It wasn't supposed to hurt this much. Jason kept his gaze fixed on the window as he heard the soft click of the door closing. He'd hoped that saying goodbye to Emily would kick-start his body and mind into forgetting her.

Forget that.

He ached all over, ached with the knowledge that he'd lost her, that he loved her.

No. He did not love Emily Wood. He would not indulge himself in that useless emotion, that recipe for unhappiness—

His childhood had been marked by his mother's sorrow, his adolescence by his father's silence. He'd seen what love did to people. How it disappointed them. And involving himself with Emily when that was what she so clearly wanted would be a very grave error. He couldn't take that risk.

Have you ever told anyone you loved them?

He wasn't going to do it again.

She stayed numb. January dragged into February, and Emily went to work and home again like an automaton, performing the necessary functions of survival without ever really engaging in anything. Somehow she managed to smile and talk and even laugh. She thought she was giving a pretty convincing performance that she was fine. And maybe, eventually, her mind and heart would be convinced as well and she'd really start living—and feeling—again.

Other people had recovered from their setbacks, Emily told herself. Helen was now happy with Richard, even though he'd gone to Brazil with Jason. Skype and email worked wonders, and her brief infatuation with Philip was clearly a thing of the past. Even Gillian Bateson was doing better; she had gained partial custody of her daughter and she'd dropped some of the lofty smugness that Emily knew had just been a way of protecting herself. Everyone had armour of some kind.

So why did she feel so stripped bare?

Why couldn't she feel *better*?

As February limped towards March and her heart continued its awful ache, Emily wondered if she ever would.

She was considering this rather dire possibility when the lights in her office flicked off. She looked up in surprise to see Isobel standing in the doorway.

'Work's over for the day,' she announced. 'I'm taking you out.'

'It's not even lunchtime—'

'Doesn't matter,' Isobel replied breezily. 'You need a break. Even your boss agreed.'

'*Jason?* He's in Brazil—'

'I emailed him and asked his permission because I knew you'd resist. He said of course.'

Just the thought that Jason had been thinking about her in some small way sent a fierce bolt of longing through her. She really was pathetic. She hadn't seen or spoken to him in over six weeks. 'Why would I ever resist an afternoon out?' Emily finally said, smiling. 'I've never been a workaholic, Izzy.'

'Because,' Isobel said, reaching for Emily's coat and thrusting it at her, 'I intend to give you the full sisterly interrogation. And by the end of the day you won't have a single secret from me.'

Emily sank back into her chair, eyeing her sister with increasing alarm. 'On second thoughts—'

'Consider yourself warned,' Isobel cut her off, holding up a finger in warning. 'I've booked the babysitter already, so no backing out, Emily. We have a reservation at one. And it's Jason's treat.'

'*Jason's?*' Emily repeated in incredulity. Another bolt of pain rocketed through her.

'Yes, he said to make sure to lunch in style.'

Emily silently digested this little bit of information, wondering why on earth Jason would offer such a thing. Was it to show how much he didn't care, or how much he did? And why would she even think he cared, when he'd made it so painfully clear that he didn't? Was she still living in pointless, impossible hope?

'I'm coming,' she said and, still rather reluctant, followed her sister out of her darkened office.

They ate at the Ivy and, while Emily toyed with her chicken, Isobel leaned over the table, her expression rather fierce and said, 'So you did love him.'

Startled, Emily looked up. For a shocked second she thought Isobel knew about Jason, but then she realised her sister was just speaking in generalities. 'Yes,' she admitted quietly. 'Did you think I didn't?'

Isobel shrugged and poured them both more wine. 'Well, you haven't had all that many relationships, have you? And the ones you have had haven't been spectacular. No one you even wanted to bring back to us.'

'No,' Emily agreed slowly, 'they weren't.' The two boyfriends she'd had seemed mere shadows compared to Jason; she could barely remember them now.

'Do you think that was on purpose?'

'Them not being spectacular?' Emily asked in surprise and then, after a moment's quiet reflection, she nodded. 'I suppose…it was safer that way. I didn't get hurt.' Disappointed, but not destroyed. Not like now.

'And now?' Isobel asked quietly.

Emily let out a small, sad sigh. 'Now I feel completely wrecked…but I'll get over it. I will.' She smiled, a gesture with more will than actual feeling behind it. 'I'll have to, won't I?'

'I'd bash his head in if I knew who it was…or I'd tell Jason to! It's someone from work, isn't it? I asked Jason if he knew who it was, but—'

'Oh, Izzy.' Emily let out a trembling laugh. 'I don't suppose he told you, did he?'

'No. He said it was your business and to butt out, actually. Typical Jason.'

'It *is* Jason.'

The look of shock on her sister's face would have been comical if Emily still didn't feel so awful. *'Jason?'* Isobel finally repeated in a hushed whisper. Emily nodded miserably and Isobel sat back in her chair. 'But…of course. That's why you were so miserable all holiday! And that's why Jason left…' Emily could practically see the wheels spinning in her sister's brain. 'But why did he break your heart?' she demanded. 'And how dare—'

'Don't.' Emily held up a hand. 'Don't drag the family into this, Izzy. This is about Jason and me.

And the simple truth is we want different things out of life.'

Isobel arched an eyebrow, clearly sceptical. 'That different?'

'Different enough.' Emily drew in a shaky breath. 'He's not interested in love, Izzy. Not the way I am.'

Isobel cocked her head. 'And how are you interested in love?'

Emily didn't want to go over the agonising details of her conversation with Jason; it had been hard enough the first time. She shook her head, meaning it as a dismissal. 'I want what Mum and Dad had. The real thing. True love.'

'How do you even remember what they had?' Isobel asked reasonably. 'You were three when Mum died, Emily.'

'I know, but you can tell how much they loved each other when Dad talks about Mum. He adored her, Isobel. He told me she was perfect—'

'And you want someone to think you're perfect?' Although her tone was gentle, the question felt like a rebuke…and all too similar to what Jason had told her.

'No, of course not—'

'In any case, it was twenty years ago, Emily. Don't you think Dad's memories might have become a bit rosier over time?'

Emily stared at her sister in shock. 'Are you saying they didn't love—'

'No, I am saying what they had was *real*. They disagreed. They argued. I can remember. Mum was a good deal more emotional than Dad. He did love her, but he didn't think she was perfect. Not when she was alive, anyway. And it wasn't roses and romance all the time either. It isn't for anyone.'

Roses and romance. It was far too close to what she'd said, what she'd felt. And maybe she had held a few naive dreams about what love really meant, but it still came down to the hard truth that Jason didn't love her. He didn't even want her to love him. No love, full stop.

'I understand what you're saying, Izzy. But I still want someone to love me and be able to say it at least, and Jason wasn't capable of that.'

'But if he shows you—'

'He didn't.' Emily spoke sharply. 'It's over, okay? Let me just recover in peace.' She placed her napkin on the table. 'Now, how about a bit of retail therapy? And you can thank Jason for me for the lunch.'

March dragged on and Emily found herself recalling her conversation with Isobel, as well as just about every moment she'd shared with Jason. She remembered little things, things she'd dismissed or forgotten that suddenly seemed important now. The way he smiled, and how sweet his touch had been. His gentle teasing, which she'd always enjoyed until her heart had got tangled up in it. She thought of how she'd always trusted him, always known he would keep her safe.

The memories ran through her head in an endless reel and left her restless and wanting, wishing she could at least see him again. Ask him…what?

What could she possibly say? *I don't care if you only love me a little bit. I don't need any grand gestures…*

But she didn't even know if he loved her at all. She was quite sure he didn't, and gestures didn't even come into it. They had no relationship. No future.

Nothing.

Jason ran his hands through his hair, every muscle in his body aching. He'd been working twelve- and fourteen-hour days in an effort to wrap up the consulting work in Brazil…and in a useless attempt to forget Emily.

It wasn't working. Even in the middle of the most complicated, mind-consuming work, she slipped into his thoughts. He could hear her laughter, picture the way her eyes glittered jade with amusement. He imagined he could smell her strawberry shampoo. And at night she came to him in his dreams. He woke up restless and painfully unfulfilled. Four months of celibacy had taken their toll on his temper to boot. His staff tiptoed around him; the only one whose mood hadn't soured was Richard, who had celebrated his engagement last night.

At least *someone* had seen sense.

The trill of his mobile had him turning away from his laptop screen, as irritable as ever. He glanced at the telephone's little screen, intending not to take the call, when he saw who it was. Isobel.

'Izzy?'

'Oh, Jason, I'm so glad I reached you.' Isobel sniffed, and with a lurch of alarm, Jason realised she must have been crying.

'What's happened? What's wrong?'

'Oh, Jason, it's…'

'Emily?' Alarm turned to panic and he felt as if his heart had stopped, suspended in his chest, refusing to beat. 'Is Emily all right?' Already he pictured her lying pale and lifeless on a stretcher, broken on a road. *Something* must have happened—

'No, no, Emily's all right. It's our father. He's had a stroke. They don't think…' Isobel swallowed. 'They don't think he'll recover. I thought you'd want to know.'

'Of course. Oh, Isobel, I'm so sorry.' He thought of Henry's kindly face, his ready smile and ever-present good humour. And then he thought of Emily, her father's spoiled darling, and he realised how agonising this must be for her. And, as he listened to Isobel give more details about Henry Wood's condition, he knew what he needed to do. What he wanted to do.

Emily stared at her father's still form on the hospital bed. He suddenly seemed so *small,* barely making a hump under the bed covers. She swallowed past the lump in her throat, her body aching with fatigue. Ever since Isobel had rung her yesterday, she'd maintained this vigil by her father's bed, praying that it might make a difference. That he might come back to them. She couldn't lose another person she loved, not like this. She rested her hand on top of his, felt the thin, papery texture of his skin. 'Oh, Daddy,' she whispered. 'Don't leave me, not yet. I love you so much.'

A nurse came in, pausing in the doorway. 'There's a visitor here, miss, but as he's not immediate family I didn't know whether—'

Emily turned to her with an audible sniff. 'Is he outside? I'll talk to him.' There had been a steady stream of well-wishers coming to visit Henry, old work colleagues and family friends, and the thought of greeting another one made her spirits dip even lower. She was tired of answering the same questions over and over when her own grief still threatened to overwhelm her.

She headed out into the fluorescent-lit hallway, blinking in the bright light. And then she thought she must be seeing things. She was tired enough to start hallucinating, and perhaps her exhausted mind had manufactured the one person she wanted to see more than anyone.

Jason stood in the hallway.

CHAPTER THIRTEEN

SHE stared at him, half-expecting him to disappear or dissolve, the product of an overtired mind—and a still-broken heart. But he didn't vanish; he was real. He came towards her, his expression serious, his arms outstretched.

'Emily, I'm so sorry about your father. I came as soon as I heard.'

And naturally, without even questioning what she was doing, Emily walked into Jason's outstretched arms. It was the only place she wanted to be. He held her, his chin resting on top of her head, his arms around her and Emily closed her eyes. It felt so good to be held like this. By Jason. 'Has there been any change?'

She shook her head, her eyes still closed. 'No… but they say there's still a chance he might recover.' Belatedly, Emily realised it was probably not a good idea to be held by Jason like this. It made too many longings rise up inside her, caused her heart to hurt with fresh, raw wounds, when it had numbed to a steady ache over the last four months.

'I thought you were in Brazil,' she said, stepping out of his arms.

'I was. I flew directly from there.'

Emily saw the shadows under his eyes, the lines of fatigue etched onto his face. 'You didn't have—'

'I know I didn't have to. I wanted to.'

She stared at him, trying to make sense of his words. And her own feelings. She'd needed him, and he'd come. She hadn't even admitted to herself that she needed him, yet somehow Jason had known. And that was better than any words he could—or couldn't—say.

'Thank you,' she said simply, because her heart was too full and fearful to say—or think—anything more.

'How is Henry?'

Jason jerked his gaze away from the darkened windows of the drawing room to gaze at his father. He'd come to Weldon directly from the hospital, but his mind was still with Emily. She'd looked so tired, so pale, so *sad*. He hated seeing her that way. 'The same. He hasn't been responsive since the stroke.'

'Will he recover, do you think?'

Jason suppressed the stab of irritation he felt at his father's dispassionate tone. Henry Wood was one of Edward Kingsley's oldest friends, yet you'd hardly know it to hear his father talk. His face was expressionless, his gaze on the fire.

'I don't know. They said it could go either way

at this point, although any recovery he has will be limited.'

Edward rubbed his jaw, his expression still inscrutable. 'Hard to believe,' he finally said. 'Makes you think.'

'Oh, does it?' Jason couldn't quite keep the sarcasm from his tone. Emily's haggard face flashed across his mind.

'Yes, it does,' Edward said. He turned to look at his son, and Jason saw a surprising bleakness in his eyes. 'Makes you look at your own life a bit, when you realise how the clock is winding down for us all. My health hasn't been good. You know that.'

Jason didn't think he'd ever heard his father speak so many words in one go. He almost sounded maudlin. 'And have you come to any conclusions?' he asked, his tone diffident.

'Not as such.' Edward glanced back at the fire. 'I suppose I have a few regrets. Things I should have said. Never did.' Each sentence was said in staccato, with clear reluctance.

Jason's body tensed, and he realised he wanted to know what his father thought he should have said over the years. He wanted to know very much, more than he'd ever realised. 'You could say them now,' he said after a moment.

Edward gave him a fleeting smile, no more than a grim twisting of his lips. 'No, I can't. The person I should have said them to is dead.'

Jason's fists clenched of their own accord. He

strove to keep his voice neutral. 'You mean my mother?'

'Yes.' Edward was silent for a long moment, gazing into the fire. 'I loved her, you know. I never said it.'

Jason made himself unclench his fists. 'Why not?'

Edward shrugged. 'I don't know. No one ever said it much to me. Wasn't the thing. And I suppose I didn't like the thought of admitting something that seemed like weakness.' He let out a long, slow breath. 'Perhaps it's weaker not to say it at all.' He faced Jason again, his expression more open and vulnerable than Jason had ever seen it. 'I can say it to you though, can't I? I never did.' Edward smiled again, even let out a little laugh. 'God knows it's still damned difficult. I love you though, Jason. I'm sorry I've never said.' He spoke gruffly, averting his head quickly, yet the words still flooded through Jason. Just words.

Powerful words. A powerful *feeling*, one that completely swept him off his feet.

Not meaningless sentiments. Not just grand gestures.

Hearing his father's simple, heartfelt statement made Jason realise the truth of his own feelings. The truth about love.

It was powerful, strong, real.

And he needed to tell Emily.

* * *

It had been a long, exhausting week. Emily cradled her mug of coffee in the kitchen of Hartington House, fatigue making her whole body ache. Yet even amidst the exhaustion she felt a sweet, sweet relief; last night her father had finally regained consciousness. It was going to be a long, arduous road, and he would never see a complete recovery. Emily knew that, had heard the specialists talk about limited speech and mobility, the use of a walker or a wheelchair. It was hard to accept that, but it was better than the alternative. It was something.

And something was enough.

Jason had visited Henry every day this week, commuting from London, and Emily had welcomed and appreciated his presence more than she could say.

She *hadn't* said, because part of her wanted to tell Jason how much he meant to her, how much she loved him. Yet surely there was no point. Jason had shown up as a family friend, nothing more. It didn't change things between them.

Except *she* felt changed. The last week—the last four months—had made her realise just how childish and naive her dreams about love had been. Love wasn't about words or gestures, it was about action. Connection.

Anyone can tell you he loves you.

But not everyone would travel thousands of miles to be with her in her moment of need. Not everyone would be so trustworthy, so solid and steady and safe… The exact thing she needed. Wanted.

Jason.

She still loved him, would always love him. Yet, even so, it didn't change how he felt. He didn't love her, and even if she could have accepted that, lived with it, she knew Jason would not accept what she had to offer.

He didn't want love. He didn't want her.

A knock on the front door jolted her out of her gloomy thoughts. Sighing, Emily prepared to accept another casserole from one of the village's well-meaning widows. She'd had no idea her father was so popular.

Yet when she opened the door, there were no widows in sight. Jason stood there, smiling. Looking wonderful.

Emily stared at him in shock. 'I thought you'd returned to London—'

'I came back.'

'Why?'

'I have something to say to you.' He suddenly looked so serious that Emily felt as if her heart had frozen in her chest. Cold and lifeless. Was he going to tell her he'd found his sensible wife at last? Was she going to have to pretend to be pleased? It had been four months, after all. Plenty of time.

Reluctantly, she moved from the doorway. 'Come in, then,' she said, knowing she sounded ungracious.

'Actually, I want you to come with me.'

Emily blinked. 'Where?'

'It's a surprise.'

A surprise? She eyed him warily. Jason didn't generally do surprises. 'I'm not sure I'm up to going anywhere, Jason. I'm expecting a call from the hospital—'

'I just checked in with the nursing station. Your father's sleeping. And we can visit him afterwards, if you like.'

'Afterwards?'

'Come on.' He smiled and tugged her hand and, still uncertain, a little suspicious and even afraid, Emily let him lead her to his Porsche.

She sneaked a glance at him as he drove; his jaw was tense, his gaze fixed straight ahead. He looked determined, fiercely so, and the thought gave her a little lurch of alarm.

They drove in silence towards London, skirting the south side of the city before heading towards Greenwich. Emily only just kept herself from asking where they were going. She wasn't sure she wanted to know.

Jason finally turned into a small park next to the Thames; the water glinted silver under the fragile spring sunlight.

'So where have you brought me?' Emily asked as she got out of the car. The wind breezing off the river blew her hair into tangles and she pushed the unruly mass back from her face.

'One of my favourite places in England,' Jason said ruefully, 'although it might not seem like very much. Walk with me.'

Obediently, Emily fell into step alongside him, her curiosity rising like a tide inside her. Why had Jason taken her to one of his favourite places? And *why* was this one of his favourite places? She glanced around; it looked like a rather bland park, nothing more than a couple of picnic tables and benches on a bit of green.

Jason stopped on the pavement that ran alongside the river and, bracing his forearms on the rails, he gestured out towards the flat expanse of water. 'There.' Emily glanced at the river; there were a few large bulky silver things positioned across the water. 'Do you know what that is?'

'Er…' She had a feeling she *should* know, considering she worked for the foremost firm in hydraulic engineering. 'Some flood…thing?'

Jason smiled faintly. 'The Thames Flood Barrier. The largest in the world. My father brought me here when it opened, when I was about ten.' Emily nodded, wondering why he'd brought *her* here, what he was going to say. 'I was fascinated by its strength,' Jason said slowly. 'Water is one of the most powerful forces in the world, and yet when these gates go up this barrier is able to stop it. Control it. I thought that was what drew me to engineering—the ability to control a powerful force. But I realise there's another side to it—the sheer power and beauty and even unpredictability of water.' He must have seen Emily's rather blank look for he laughed softly and said, 'I'm not making much sense, am I? And here I was, trying to say something romantic about love and how it overwhelmed me, a far more powerful force than any river.'

'*Love?*' Emily echoed in both disbelief and dawning hope. 'I'm afraid I didn't get that at all.'

'I told you I wasn't good at this.'

'Good at what?'

'Grand gestures. Words. Three words in particular.'

Emily's heart seemed to stop right in her chest, as if a huge fist had clenched around it. 'And here I thought you were wittering on about flood barriers,' she managed weakly.

'Waxing poetically, actually.' He glanced at his watch. 'Ah, just about time.'

'Time for what?'

He pointed upwards and Emily looked uncomprehendingly at the pale blue sky, a few fleecy clouds scudding across its surface. 'What...?' And then she saw the plane cutting across the blue, making recognisable loops. Spelling letters.

'Sky writing?' she exclaimed, and Jason smiled self-consciously.

'To be honest, I didn't know if you'd go for it. But I wanted to make a statement.'

She watched in silence as the plane spelled the words, words she'd longed to hear. *I. Love. You.* She turned to him, hope and disbelief warring within her. 'Jason—'

'Of course I can't take the easy way out and let that do the talking for me,' he said, pointing to the words emblazoned in smoke across the sky. 'I need to say it myself. I want to, because God knows I feel it. And that's what I *didn't* want, what I've been fighting against for a long time now.' Emily waited, her heart seeming to squeeze inside her chest, as Jason turned to her, smiling although his eyes were dark and serious. 'I love you, Emily. And loving you means loving all of you, including the part of you that wanted more from me than I was willing to give.'

She stared at him, her mind dazed and body rocked by this admission. 'But all I wanted was you to love me, Jason,' she whispered. 'And I didn't think you did—'

'I didn't want to,' Jason admitted. 'Loving someone is, I've discovered, scary. You open yourself up to all sorts of risk and hurt.'

'I know.' Did she ever. She'd felt the same way… even if she'd expressed it differently.

'I'd convinced myself for so long that I didn't want it, wasn't capable of it,' Jason continued. 'Just like my father.'

'What made you change your mind?' Emily whispered.

'You did. Wanting you, just being with you. I still fought it, of course. I'm stubborn.' He smiled wryly before his expression grew serious again. 'But you gave me a wake-up call when you asked me if I'd ever told someone I loved them, and I was going to tell you I hadn't. Of course I hadn't.' He shook his head in memory. 'And then I suddenly remembered telling my mother I loved her. She'd been crying because she was so unhappy with my father, feeling he never loved her, always wanting more. She was depressed, I realise that now, but as a child…I just wanted to make her feel better.' He let out a shaky breath. 'So I told her I loved her, and that night she killed herself.'

Emily let out a little gasp of shock. She'd had no idea Jason lived with a memory like that, felt its terrible pain through the years. 'I'm sorry—'

'So am I. Sorry for my mother, who was so desperately unhappy, and sorry that her experience—and mine as a child—made me doubt the power of love and only acknowledge its pain. I convinced myself that loving someone was a bad idea. That words and gestures could never be enough, just like my father's love wasn't enough for my mother. Like my words—my love—hadn't been enough.'

'Oh, Jason—'

'So I convinced myself I wanted a convenient marriage on both sides because I didn't want anyone to be disappointed, but I see now I was just protecting myself from being hurt. But it didn't work, of course, because love is like that water out there.' He gestured to the river. 'An unstoppable force.' He reached for her, his arms coming around her, drawing her to him. Emily went into the embrace, dazed, still disbelieving. 'My heart has no flood barrier,' Jason said softly. 'And love—*you*—overwhelmed me.'

'I did?'

'Yes, with your warmth and your openness and your sexy shoes.'

Emily let out a laugh of incredulity. 'I thought you hated my shoes.'

'They drove me crazy. You drove me crazy. I couldn't keep away from you. I still can't. I can't believe I waited this long to finally admit how much I love you.'

Emily let out a trembling laugh. 'And I was just trying to convince myself I didn't need you to love me.'

'What?' Jason stared at her in surprise. 'Why not?'

'Because I love you so much. And when you showed up at the hospital, and I knew you'd come all that way because you knew I needed you…well, that meant more to me than any…any plastic-wrapped bouquets or meaningless sentiments!'

Jason laughed wryly. 'I really have been an awful cynic.'

'And I've been a bit silly about what I thought love needed to be,' Emily said, reaching up to caress his cheek, needing to touch him. 'Thinking it was all about the roses and romance. And there I was, trying to tell you I was an expert.'

'I think love has a habit of knocking you for six.' He drew her to him, tilting her face up to his. 'Sweeping you off your feet, as a matter of fact.' He kissed her then, the feel of his lips so sweet and warm and *perfect*. 'I love you, Emily,' Jason said as he gazed down at her. 'You are warm and generous and impulsive and emotional—'

'Even though I've been a bit of an idiot?' Emily said. 'I didn't even know what love really meant—'

'I've been an idiot for four months. I could have solved all this a lot sooner if I hadn't fought against the thought of loving you so much.'

'You love me,' Emily said slowly, wonderingly, for she still felt as if she ought to pinch herself.

'Yes. I love you, Emily Wood. I think I've loved you for years. I certainly couldn't forget that dance.'

'I felt such a fool—'

'And I was the bigger fool. I thought I knew what I needed, but all I've ever needed is you. And now it's time for my grand gesture.' Smiling, his eyes alight with both mischief and love, Jason dropped to one knee. Emily's heart seemed to freeze in her chest before it did a complete somersault. She watched him take a small black velvet box out of his pocket and flip it open to reveal the most exquisite antique ring, a diamond nestled amidst a cluster of sapphires. 'Emily Wood, I love you madly, deeply, completely. Will you be my wife and make a go of it with me?'

Emily burst out laughing, the sound one of utter joy. 'Yes, I will,' she said, pulling on his hands to get him to rise. Jason slid the ring on her finger, the diamond sparkling in the sunlight. 'I will be overjoyed to make a go of it with you.'

'Music to my ears,' Jason murmured, and pulled her closer for a kiss that made Emily's head spin and her heart overflow.

She pulled him closer, her fingers threading through his hair, her body pressed to his as joy filled and overwhelmed her. Beside them, the waters of the river flowed past the flood barrier, sparkling and silver, a beautiful, powerful force, forever surging onwards.

LARGER-PRINT BOOKS!

GET 2 FREE LARGER-PRINT NOVELS PLUS 2 FREE GIFTS!